The Christmas Program

"Grandma, it's the program tonight."

Waving away her own forgetfulness, she said, "Well, then, you better wear this." She produced something from a big apron pocket. It looked like a coil of baling wire.

She handed it over. It was a coil of baling wire. Twisted in it were tiny tin stars, cut from cans. A day's work to make. Grandma stood back, her hands clasped, a little eagerness in her eyes. "Watch out them stars don't dig your scalp."

She'd made me a halo so Carleen Lovejoy in all her tinsel wouldn't outshine me. It looked more like a crown of thorns, but I handled it, carefully.

I'd have come dangerously near to kissing Grandma then, if she'd let me.

Also by Richard Peck

OTHER PUFFIN BOOKS YOU MAY ENJOY

A Year Down Yonder

RICHARD PECK

PUFFIN BOOKS

PUFFIN BOOKS

Published by the Penguin Group

Penguin Putnam Books for Young Readers,

345 Hudson Street, New York, New York 10014, U.S.A.

Penguin Books Ltd, 80 Strand, London WC2R ORL, England

Penguin Books Australia Ltd, Ringwood, Victoria, Australia

Penguin Books Canada Ltd, 10 Alcorn Avenue, Toronto, Ontario, Canada M4V 3B2

Penguin Books (N.Z.) Ltd, 182-190 Wairau Road, Auckland 10, New Zealand

Penguin Books Ltd, Registered Offices: Harmondsworth, Middlesex, England

First published in the United States of America by Dial Books for Young Readers,
a division of Penguin Putnam Books for Young Readers, 2000
Published by Puffin Books,
a division of Penguin Putnam Books for Young Readers, 2002

5 7 9 10 8 6

THE LIBRARY OF CONGRESS HAS CATALOGED THE DIAL EDITION AS FOLLOWS:
Peck, Richard, date.
A year down yonder / Richard Peck.
p.   cm.
Sequel to: A long way from Chicago.
Summary: During the recession of 1937, fifteen-year-old Mary Alice is sent to
live with her feisty, larger-than-life grandmother in rural Illinois and
comes to a better understanding of this fearsome woman.
ISBN 0-8037-2518-3 (hc)
[1. Grandmothers—Fiction. 2. Country life—Illinois—Fiction. 3. Illinois—Fiction.]
I. Title.
PZ7.P338Yh 2000 [Fic]—dc21 99-34159 CIP

Puffin Books ISBN 0-14-230070-5

Printed in the United States of America

To the Talberts—
Moo and Marc, Molly and Jessie.

CONTENTS

—

Prologue

It was a September morning, hazy with late summer, and now with all the years between. Mother was seeing me off at Dearborn Station in Chicago. We'd come in a taxicab because of my trunk. But Mother would ride back home on the El. There wasn't much more than a nickel in her purse, and only a sandwich for the train in mine. My ticket had pretty well cleaned us out.

The trunk, a small one, held every stitch of clothes I had and two or three things of Mother's that fit me. "Try not to grow too fast," she murmured. "But anyway, skirts are shorter this year."

Then we couldn't look at each other. I was fifteen, and

I'd been growing like a weed. My shoes from Easter gripped my feet.

A billboard across from the station read:

WASN'T THE DEPRESSION AWFUL?

This was to make us think the hard times were past. But now in 1937 a recession had brought us low again. People were beginning to call it the Roosevelt recession.

Dad lost his job, so we'd had to give up the apartment. He and Mother were moving into a "light housekeeping" room. They could get it for seven dollars a week, with kitchen privileges, but it was only big enough for the two of them.

My brother Joey—Joe—had been taken on by the Civilian Conservation Corps to plant trees out west. That left me, Mary Alice. I wished I was two years older and a boy. I wished I was Joey.

But I wasn't, so I had to go down to live with Grandma Dowdel, till we could get on our feet as a family again. It meant I'd have to leave my school. I'd have to enroll in the hick-town school where Grandma lived. Me, a city girl, in a town that didn't even have a picture show.

It meant I'd be living with Grandma. No telephone, of course. And the attic was spooky and stuffy, and you had to go outdoors to the privy. Nothing modern. Everything as old as Grandma. Some of it older.

Now they were calling the train, and my eyes got blurry. Always before, Joey and I had gone to Grandma's for a week in the summer. Now it was just me. And at the other end of the trip—Grandma.

Mother gave me a quick squeeze before she let me go. And I could swear I heard her murmur, "Better you than me."

She meant Grandma.

Rich Chicago Girl

Oh, didn't I feel sorry for myself when the Wabash Railroad's Blue Bird train steamed into Grandma's town. The sandwich was still crumbs in my throat because I didn't have the dime for a bottle of pop. They wanted a dime for pop on the train.

My trunk thumped out onto the platform from the baggage car ahead. There I stood at the end of the world with all I had left. Bootsie and my radio.

Bootsie was my cat, with a patch of white fur on each paw. She'd traveled in a picnic hamper. Bootsie had come from down here, two summers ago when she was a kitten. Now she was grown but scrawny. She'd spent the trip trying to claw through the hamper. She didn't like change any more than I did.

My portable radio was in my other hand. It was a Philco with a leatherette cover and handle. Portable radios weighed ten pounds in those days.

As the train pulled out behind me, there came Grandma up the platform steps. My goodness, she was a big woman. I'd forgotten. And taller still with her spidery old umbrella held up to keep off the sun of high noon. A fan of white hair escaped the big bun on the back of her head. She drew nearer till she blotted out the day.

You couldn't call her a welcoming woman, and there wasn't a hug in her. She didn't put out her arms, so I had nothing to run into.

Nobody had told Grandma that skirts were shorter this year. Her skirttails brushed her shoes. I recognized the dress. It was the one she put on in hot weather to walk uptown in. Though I was two years older, two years taller than last time, she wasn't one for personal comments. The picnic hamper quivered, and she noticed. "What's in there?"

"Bootsie," I said. "My cat."

"Hoo-boy," Grandma said. "Another mouth to feed." Her lips pleated. "And what's that thing?" She nodded to my other hand.

"My radio." But it was more than a radio to me. It was my last touch with the world.

5

"That's all we need." Grandma looked skyward. "More noise."

She aimed one of her chins down the platform. "That yours?" She meant the trunk. It was the footlocker Dad had brought home from the Great War.

"Leave it," she said. "They'll bring it to the house." She turned and trudged away, and I was supposed to follow. I walked away from my trunk, wondering if I'd ever see it again. It wouldn't have lasted long on the platform in Chicago. Hot tongs wouldn't have separated me from Bootsie and my radio.

The recession of thirty-seven had hit Grandma's town harder than it had hit Chicago. Grass grew in the main street. Only a face or two showed in the window of The Coffee Pot Cafe. Moore's Store was hurting for trade. Weidenbach's bank looked to be just barely in business.

On the other side of the weedy road, Grandma turned the wrong way, away from her house. Two old slab-sided dogs slept on the sidewalk. Bootsie knew because she was having a conniption in the hamper. And my radio was getting heavier. I caught up with Grandma.

"Where are we going?"

"Going?" she said, the picture of surprise. "Why, to school. You've already missed pretty nearly two weeks."

"School!" I'd have clutched my forehead if my hands weren't full. "On my first day here?"

Grandma stopped dead and spoke clear. "You're going to school. I don't want the law on me."

"Grandma, the law's afraid of you. You'd grab up that

6

shotgun from behind the woodbox if the sheriff came on your place."

It was true. The whole town knew Grandma was trigger-happy.

"Well, I don't want it to come to that." She trudged on.

I could have broken down and bawled then. Bootsie in her hamper, banging my knees. The sun beating down like it was still summer. I could have flopped in the weeds and cried my eyes out. But I thought I better not.

Under a shade tree just ahead was a hitching rail. Tied to it were some mostly swaybacked horses and a mule or two that the country kids rode to school. One horse was like another to me, but Grandma stopped to look them over.

There was a big gray with a tangled tail, switching flies. Grandma examined him from stem to stern. I thought she might pry his jaws apart for a look at his teeth. She took her time looking, though I was in no hurry.

Then on she went across a bald yard to the school. It was wooden-sided with a bell tower. I sighed.

On either side of the school was an outdoor privy. One side for the boys, one for the girls. Labeled. And a pump.

Grandma slowed again as the bell tower rose above us. She'd never been to high school. She'd been expelled from a one-room schoolhouse long before eighth grade. I happened to know this.

Crumbling steps led up to a front entrance. Somebody had scrawled a poem all over the door:

> Ashes to ashes,
> Dust to dust,
> Oil them brains
> Before they rust.

Steps led down to the basement under the front stoop. Grandma went down there, closing her umbrella.

The basement was one big room. A basketball hoop hung at either end, but it didn't look like a gym to me. Smelled like one, though.

A tall, hollow-cheeked man leaned on a push broom in the center of the floor.

"Well, August!" Grandma boomed, and the room echoed.

This woke him up. When he saw Grandma, he swallowed hard. People often did. He wore old sneakers and a rusty black suit under a shop apron. His necktie was fraying at the knot.

"I've brought this girl to be enrolled." Grandma indicated me with a thumb. She didn't say I was her granddaughter. She never told more than the minimum.

I stood there, fifteen, trying to die of shame. Grandma didn't understand about high school. She was trying to get the janitor to enroll me.

But I had it all wrong. They'd fired the janitor when times got hard. August—Mr. Fluke—*was* the principal, which made him the coach too. And he taught shop to the boys. And swept up.

"Well, Mrs. Dowdel," the principal said, "can this girl read and cipher?" Even I saw he was pulling Grandma's leg, which never worked.

"Good enough to get by in a school like this," she replied.

Mr. Fluke turned to me. "Mary Alice, is it? Down from Chicago?" Everybody in this town knew everything about you. They knew things that hadn't even happened yet. "What grade did they have you in up there?"

"Would have been tenth," I mumbled. "Sophomore."

"Let's call that junior year down here," Mr. Fluke said. "It don't matter, and there's plenty of room for you. High school's getting to be a luxury in times like these. So many boys have dropped out entirely, I don't know where I'll find five to play basketball, come winter, or to field the Christmas program."

The thought of winter—Christmas—here chilled my heart.

"Oh, we'll pull a couple of the farm boys back after they get the last of the hay in," Mr. Fluke went on. "But some of 'em won't drift back to school till that last ear of corn is picked in November. You know boys."

Grandma nodded. "Boys is bad business," she said, quite agreeable for her. "Though girls is worse."

But Grandma never had time to waste visiting. Shortly Mr. Fluke was sending us up to Miss Butler's classroom. It was at the top of some rickety stairs. At the front of the room, Miss Butler was reading aloud:

> *For never was a story of more woe*
> *Than this of Juliet and her Romeo.*

Oh woe. Shakespeare even here. My heart sank to my shoes. But it sounded like they were coming to the end.

From out in the hall Grandma and I saw that the students sat two-by-two in old-timey double desks. One girl sat alone. Grandma nudged me. "See that big girl with the dirty hair?"

You couldn't miss her. "Who is she?"

"One of the Burdick girls. Mildred, I think. They're kin of the Eubankses. Steer clear of her if you can. Watch your back if you can't."

"What's wrong with her?"

"She's a Burdick."

But then Grandma was pushing me forward. Somehow she'd taken Bootsie and the radio out of my hands. My hands were like ice. I teetered on the threshold. When Grandma loomed up behind me, all three boys in the classroom threw up their hands and hollered out, "Don't shoot! We give up!"

Which is a boy's idea of trying to be funny. I personally thought they ought to show more respect for an old lady, even if it was Grandma.

Miss Butler saw us and clapped a hand against her

straight bosom. "Oh hark," she said. "It's Mrs. Dowdel, and . . ."

"Mary Alice Dowdel," I said in a wobbly voice. "I'm enrolled."

"Well, how . . . nice," Miss Butler said, avoiding Grandma's eye. "Boys and girls, this is Mary Alice Dowdel, come down to us from Chicago. I guess times are hard up there too."

There was absolutely no privacy in a town this size. I saw how hard Grandma had to work to keep people's noses out of her business. I looked back at her and she was gone.

"Mary Alice, honey," Miss Butler was saying, "you can share with Mildred Burdick until we find you some schoolbooks. Mildred, move over and make Mary Alice welcome."

The day went straight downhill from there.

Mildred Burdick took up more than her share of the seat. And she didn't look any better up close. While Miss Butler bustled at the blackboard, Mildred looked me over, and she didn't like what she saw. She started with the top of my head. Mother had given me a finger wave, and it was real tight from a center parting.

Mildred's lip curled.

For traveling, I had on my second-best summer cotton, the one with the puff sleeves and the three big celluloid buttons off one of Mother's dresses. Mildred looked at my puff sleeves like they ought to come off.

Then she dipped down for a look at my feet. I had on my Easter shoes with the open toes, and bobby socks.

Mildred made a little buzz-saw sound in her throat that would have worried anybody. I didn't want to stare at what she was wearing. It seemed to be a lumberjack shirt. She smelled real warm. I felt eyes on me from all over the room. Everybody was watching.

"I'll make ya welcome," Mildred rasped. She made a big fist and showed it to me, under the desk. "Rich Chicago girl."

I sighed. "If I was rich, I wouldn't be here."

Now Mildred was in my face. She had one blue eye and one green. Burdicks did, but I didn't know that then, and it was distracting. "Where'd ya get that dress?" Her breath took mine away.

"Mother made it," I said. "From a Butterick pattern."

"You wear a thing like that to school up in Chicago?"

I nodded, helpless.

"How big is that school up in Chicago?"

"I don't know. About a thousand kids." I wondered if Miss Butler was ever going to turn around from the blackboard.

Mildred's eerie eyes widened. "Liar," she said. "Ya owe me a dollar, rich Chicago girl."

Now somebody tapped my arm, just below that puff sleeve. A starved-looking girl with big eyes was leaning across from her desk. I didn't know her, of course, but she turned out to be Ina-Rae Gage. Her lips were in my ear.

"Don't mess with Mildred," she said moistly. "She ate my lunch."

"She wants a dollar," I whispered back.

"Don't cross her. Better settle with her," Ina-Rae whispered in return. "She'll foller you home. She does that."

Mildred jabbed me. Her arms were big, but her elbow was sharp. "Ya owe me a buck," she reminded. "And I ain't afraid of your grandma. Ya oughtta see mine. Mine drinks straight from the bottle and wears tar all over to keep off the fleas. And my paw's meaner than a snake. He's tougher than any of them Chicago gangsters. He's worse than Pretty Boy Floyd, and lots uglier."

I didn't doubt it.

At last, Miss Butler turned around. "Take out your history books, boys and girls," she trilled. "Hop to it like bedbugs!"

"I thought this was English class," I whispered across to Ina-Rae. "Wasn't that Shakespeare?"

"Who?" Ina-Rae said.

But I was to learn that we had English and history and geography from Miss Butler. Then we went across the hall and had math and science from Mr. Herkimer. He taught the boys Ag. and Miss Butler taught Home Ec. to the girls. We were back and forth. And this wasn't the junior class. It was half the school. Ina-Rae was a freshman. What Mildred was, nobody knew. I sighed all afternoon.

When school finally let out, Mildred marched me

over to the hitching rail. All twenty-five of the students in high school milled in the yard. The boys were pegging out a game of horseshoes. But there was no help in sight for me. Everybody looked the other way.

Somehow Mildred seemed even bigger outdoors. She wore overalls under a snagged skirt because she rode a horse to school. It was the big gray with the twitching tail that had interested Grandma. And I have to say, Mildred's horse was better-looking than she was.

For a terrible moment I thought she was going to make me ride up behind her. That horse looked sky high. But she said, briefly, "I ride. You walk."

Right through the town we went, me in the dust of the road, ahead of the slobbering horse, Mildred riding astride like a bounty hunter.

Grandma lived at the other end of town in the last house. She was sitting out in the swing on her back porch, though as a rule she kept busier than that. It almost looked like she was waiting for us.

I came dragging into the side yard with Mildred's horse behind me. And Mildred. I guess I was glad to see Grandma there on the porch. I don't know. I was pretty near the end of my rope.

Mildred dropped down and tied her horse to a tree. Grandma was on her feet now. The swing swayed behind her. At the foot of the porch steps I stared at the ground and said, "Mildred says I owe her a dollar."

"Do tell." Grandma stroked her big cheek. She looked down at me over her spectacles. "You run up quite a big bill for your first day. A buck's a week's wages around here. Two weeks' for a Burdick."

Mildred stood her ground behind me. I could feel her breath on my neck. She was tough. Not too bright, but tough.

"Well, come on in the house," Grandma said. "We'll talk it over." She turned back to the screen door. "Get them boots off." She pointed to Mildred's. "They're caked with something I don't want on my kitchen floor."

Mildred's eyes flashed two colors. But Grandma was bigger than she was. She squatted to unlace her boots. Then she stood them by the back door.

We went inside. Without her boots, Mildred had lost some steam. Her socks were more hole than cotton. This may have been the first clean kitchen of her experience. She looked around, wary. But not wary enough.

"How about a glass of buttermilk to wet your whistles?" Grandma had been making cottage cheese. A big cloth sack of clabber dripped into a bowl. She waved us into chairs.

I could take buttermilk or leave it. Mildred guzzled hers. It left her with a white mustache, and a little more of her authority slipped away. Grandma cut us two big squares of cold corn bread out of a pan.

"How's your Grandma Idella?" Grandma said to Mildred, friendly as anything. "I hear she's had the dropsy and she's too puny to get off the bed."

"She's poorly," Mildred admitted. "She's pinin' and fixin' to give out."

"Poor old soul," Grandma said. "I'll get a jar of my huckleberry jam out of the cellar for her. I expect she can keep that down."

Grandma's spectacled gaze grazed me as she sailed out the back door. She was up to something. She didn't have to go outdoors to go down her cellar. The cellar door was right behind my chair.

Mildred wolfed the corn bread, though she'd eaten Ina-Rae's lunch.

Grandma was soon back, without the huckleberry jam. I don't remember her ever making huckleberry jam.

"And is your paw still in the penitentiary?" she asked Mildred.

"He was framed," Mildred mumbled, sulky.

"Oh, I guess them sheep off the Bowman farm found their own way into your pen." Grandma stood at her ease before the black iron range. It was her usual spot. The linoleum there was worn to the floorboards.

"Mildred's paw's a famous horse trader in these parts," Grandma explained to me, "when he's not in the clink. People still talk about how he sold that half-dead nag to Old Man Nyquist. Mildred's paw fed a live eel down that plug horse's throat. It was lively as a young colt for the time it took to sell it to Nyquist. Of course, when the eel died, that old crowbait nag lost all its get-up-an'-go. Nyquist had to send it to the scavenger."

"I don't know nothin' about that," said Mildred with her mouth full.

But I was suddenly arrested by a sight that only Grandma and I saw. Mildred couldn't see it. Her back was to the door. Her big gray horse was trotting away, past the porch, free as air. Tied around its neck were Mildred's boots. I nearly fell off the chair in surprise. But Grandma gazed into space, seeming to count the cadavers on her flypaper strip.

Presently she said to Mildred, "We'll talk about that dollar another time. You better get on your way. You've got five miles of bad road ahead of you. You won't be home till pretty nearly midnight."

Mildred looked up. Whatever she saw in Grandma's eyes brought her out of her chair. It tipped over behind her. Mildred pounded sock-footed out onto the back porch. The horse was gone. When she grabbed for her boots, they were gone too. She tore off the porch, heading for the road, looking both ways. But the horse was out of sight. Grandma latched the screen door behind her.

I'd never budged. Grandma righted Mildred's chair and sat down, to take the weight off her feet. Her thoughts seemed to wander, and she was using a toothpick. Grandma carried a toothpick hidden in her mouth. She could flip it forward with her tongue to pick her teeth.

At last she said, "Them Burdicks isn't worth the powder and shot to blow them up. They're like a pack of hound dogs. They'll chase livestock, suck eggs, and lick the skillet. And steal? They'd steal a hot stove and come back for the smoke."

"Grandma," I said, "you'll get me killed. She wants a dollar off me. Instead, you untied her horse and slung her boots around its neck and she has to walk home."

"Barefoot," Grandma said.

"Grandma, tomorrow at school she'll take it out of my hide."

"She won't be in school tomorrow," Grandma said.

"I don't see why not. She'll ride to school tomorrow just to skin me alive."

"No, she won't," Grandma said. "That horse went home. I know that horse. It belongs to the Sensenbaughs. They live seven miles in the other direction, way over there past Milmine. A horse'll go home if it gets the chance."

"You mean—"

"Mildred's paw stole every horse he ever had. And he won't steal another till he gets out of the penitentiary. I don't picture Mildred walkin' five miles both ways for an education."

". . . Barefoot," I said.

"Barefoot," Grandma said. "I can't fight all your battles for you, but I can give you a level start."

A silence fell while I thought that over. Then I said, "And you acted real nice to her too, Grandma. You gave her buttermilk and that big slab of corn bread."

"Oh well." Grandma waved herself away. "Didn't want to send her off hungry. I knew she had a long walk ahead of her."

We sat there at the kitchen table, Grandma and I, while the shadows crept across the linoleum.

In this busy day I hadn't had time to be homesick. But I thought about my brother. Joey. Always before, he'd come down here to Grandma's with me, and stuck up for me. Now he was out west, planting trees, living in a tent. I thought about Joey, and Grandma was thinking about him too. I could tell.

Then I smacked my forehead, remembering Bootsie. "Grandma! Where's Bootsie?"

"Who?"

"Bootsie, Grandma. My *cat*."

"I won't have a cat in the house," she said. "They shed. She's out in the cobhouse where she belongs."

I sank in the chair. "Grandma, she won't know where she is. She'll be scared. She'll run away. She'll try to go home like Mildred's horse."

"No, she won't," Grandma said. "I buttered her paws."

"You *what?*"

"I rubbed butter on all four of her paws. That's what you do with a cat in a new place. By the time they've licked off all that butter, they're right at home. Works every time."

"Oh, Grandma," I said, too worried to stir.

Now it was nearly evening. The sun setting down the west window glinted off Grandma's spectacles. The toothpick made little lazy revolutions between her wrinkled lips. Something thumped out on the porch. They'd brought my trunk from the depot, and what a final sound that thump was.

Then Grandma said in a thoughtful voice, "And you better settle in too, girl. Or I'll butter *your* paws."

I just sat there without a sigh left in me. But I was past bawling now as Grandma began to edge out of her chair. "How about some supper? My stomach's flapping against my backbone," she said. "If I don't eat, I get cranky."

And heaven knows, we couldn't have that.

Vittles and Vengeance

I little knew what a big holiday Halloween was in a town like Grandma's. Up in Chicago we didn't make much of it. A little trick-or-treating in a sheet. Maybe a cardboard jack-o'-lantern from Woolworth's with a candle inside if your apartment windows faced the street. But that was about the size of it.

Down here it went on for weeks, worse on the weekends. By the time Columbus Day was over, half the privies in town were uprooted and laid flat. One morning we came to school to find a complete old-fashioned buggy up on the bell tower, swinging from an axle.

I expected Grandma to be a target. Old people in big

houses were. But then Grandma wasn't just any old person. What the Halloweeners didn't know was that Halloween was her favorite holiday. And being mostly boys, they didn't seem to remember this lesson from year to year.

The fall was Grandma's favorite season. She liked laying in her supplies for cold weather. As soon as the first hard frost struck her garden, she foraged farther from home. She was like a big, bushy-tailed squirrel in an apron, gathering against the long winter.

Halloween fell on a Sunday that year, and there was to be a school party on Saturday night for the entire community. It was a typical school plan to keep us out of mischief. When Grandma heard about it, she said, "If they bob for apples, bring home two or three. We'll bake 'em with brown sugar."

Being fifteen, I didn't tell Grandma any more about high school than I could help. But she always knew everything anyway, so I showed her a notice from the principal, Mr. Fluke. The grammar in it was good, so Miss Butler must have ghostwritten it. She asked parents to provide party refreshments. In those times people turned out in droves if there was anything to eat.

"Vittles," Grandma said, scanning Miss Butler's appeal. "That'll mean pies."

"Gooseberry?" I asked. She was famous for her gooseberry pie.

But she waved me away. "You don't make a pie out of canned fruit until the dead of winter when you don't have any choice." She spoke of the winter ahead as a war she'd be waging. I must have pictured the two of us in an igloo, spearing fish through the ice. "Punkin and pecan," she said, "and we're going to be busy night and day. Girl, I hope you remember something about rolling out pie crust."

We were just finished with supper. Now I slipped away from the table with a crumbling baking powder biscuit in my pocket. Grandma and I had been having a battle about Bootsie. Grandma had never heard of cat food in a can. And there were precious few table scraps around here. She said cats were natural hunters and Bootsie could find her own meals. Cats are like the Burdicks, she said. They'd eat anything they could bite.

It was true. Bootsie had begun to forget she was a city cat. She'd settled down in the cobhouse and was growing sleek and round from a diet of birds and field mice and things I didn't want to think about.

But I hated to see her get this independent. Most evenings I'd sneak a treat from my plate out to her. She often waited on the porch with her head cocked. Grandma knew. She had eyes in the back of her head.

Tonight, though, Bootsie wasn't on the porch. There I was with a baking powder biscuit coming apart in my pocket. Then I heard a little sound, over by the spirea bushes. It was a clunking sound, followed by a small, piteous cry.

I hoped it wasn't Bootsie and knew it was. I strained to see across the dark yard. Two green eyes caught the light from the kitchen. I called her and she came, or tried to. Bootsie bounded forward, then fell back and ran a circle around herself. I was down in the yard now, scooping her up. She clawed my shoulder and quivered. When I lifted her, a nasty old rusted-out tin can was tied tight to her tail by a length of twine.

Though she wasn't allowed in the kitchen, I marched inside, holding her high. "Grandma! Look at this." The can swung below Bootsie, and her tail looked all pinched. "If this is Halloween around here," I said, "I don't like it."

Grandma just pursed her lips and took a pair of shears to the twine. "Now turn her out," she said, pointing to the door. Grandma went back to the range to stir something. The kitchen was filling up with a terrible smell. Reluctantly, I spilled Bootsie out onto the back porch. When I turned around, the smell from the pan on the stove was enough to skin my eyes.

"Grandma, what *is* that?"

"Glue. Best glue you ever used, better than store-bought. It'll bond wood to wood, metal to metal, and stay stuck till kingdom come." She turned, gasping, from the stove. Her spectacles had steamed up, and her cheeks were wet. "We'll need some picture wire." She nodded to a drawer. "And a hammer. Not the tack hammer. The big one. And there's a railroad spike around here somewheres."

I knew not to ask. It was just better to go along with her.

By and by, we were trooping off the back porch, bundled up. I wore my plaid coat from last winter, which was short in the sleeves. It was a frosty night, with a ring around the moon. Grandma and I were shadows casting shadows down her back walk, past her sleeping garden and the clothesline.

"Busy, busy, busy," Grandma muttered to herself. "Too much to do." She carried the pan of glue. I carried the rest.

The cobhouse where Bootsie lived stood facing the privy at the end of the back walk. A Japanese lantern vine that grew up over the privy rattled in the night wind. Grandma's privy was among the last left standing. The Halloweeners had struck as near as next door. That privy was just kindling now, scattered. And a plank with two holes in it, hanging down from the fence.

Setting down the smoldering glue, Grandma took the spike out of my hand. With two almighty hammer blows she drove it into the ground beside the cobhouse door. Winding the wire around the spike, she stretched it tight across the walk to tie it to the trunk of the Japanese lantern vine, about five inches off the ground. She was grunting and bent double.

"Find us a couple crates to sit on in there." She nodded to the cobhouse. "This could take a while."

The cobhouse was where Grandpa Dowdel had stored everything he'd ever owned. There was just room enough for Grandma and me on our crates, inside by the doorway. The pan of glue cooled at her feet. Bootsie found us. Though she didn't like the glue smell, she sprang onto my lap, nuzzling for the baking powder biscuit. I doled it out to her and held her close to keep my hands warm.

It was so quiet, you could hear Bootsie chew, and from miles away came the mournful whistle of a freight train. But we were silent as the tomb. Nothing could seem more deserted than this cobhouse, that privy.

At last we heard them. Bumbling boys in a bunch, making their way down past the garden. Oh, how quiet they thought they were being, with their boot heels ringing on the walk and their noisy breathing. I tried to count heads, though it was too dark to see whose. There may have been only three, though they seemed like more. In my lap Bootsie was as still as a little statue. Beside me, Grandma was at one with the darkness.

We no sooner saw the first boy than the invisible wire caught him at the ankle. He pitched forward, and a word I can't repeat burst out of him. He fell like a tree and measured his full length on the concrete walk. Nothing broke his fall but his nose.

There was scrambling. The boys behind him tried to stop, not knowing where their leader had gone. They only wondered for a moment.

Grandma lunged. As big as the cobhouse doorway, she surged through it. Moonlight struck her snow-white hair, and she looked eight feet tall. She'd have given a coroner a coronary. As the fallen boy raised his dazed head, she turned the pan of glue over on it. The glue was cool now and would set later.

He screamed, of course, and this too panicked the others. They ran into each other and the cobhouse wall. They tried to get away from Grandma. They may have thought she was a restless spirit. In a way, she was. They jibbered.

You'd think they'd cut and run back the way they came. But no. They trampled the fallen boy and hit the back fence running. He came up in a painful crouch and crippled after them. He went over the fence, and his big, galooty legs waved in the night air. Then he lit on the other side, again face first from the sound of it.

Silence fell. So much had happened in so short a time. Bootsie vanished from my lap. I joined Grandma. A wreath of steam rose from her heavy breathing into the hazy night. The walk was littered with things that seemed to have fallen off the Halloweeners.

Grandma bent down and fetched up a knife. She switched it open, and the blade gleamed. By the light of the ringed moon she read out the initials carved in its handle. "There's an A and an F and a J and an R," she read, squinting. "Do tell."

It was the kind of knife a boy likes, and Grandma approved of it too. She closed the blade and stuffed it in her pocket. "And looky there." It was a narrow-nosed handsaw, useful for sawing through a privy's posts, handy to carry. "That cost good money," she said, collecting it. We found a sack still half full of flour, abandoned by the walk. It was flour for mixing with water to mess on porches, and maybe cats. "That'll do for our pies," she said, so I gathered it up.

"I'll leave this wire stretched till morning. Watch your step on the way to the house," Grandma said. "I'll be along in a little while."

She meant she was going to use her privy, and she spoke with some satisfaction because it was still there to use.

At school the next morning, we were short of boys. Of course we'd been short of boys all along—only six or eight. And there were seventeen of us girls. But even when I counted in both rooms that morning, I only came up with three—Elmo Leaper and the two Johnson brothers. And they weren't town boys. They were country boys—boots and bib overalls.

Nobody mentioned the absentees. At least nobody mentioned them to me. But like Grandma herself, I wasn't the first one people ran to with news.

Anybody who thinks small towns are friendlier than big cities lives in a big city. Except for Ina-Rae Gage, they were all giving me a wide berth. The leader of the girls was clearly Carleen Lovejoy, the grain dealer's daughter. She was about as stuck-up as she could be, in the circumstances. If she bothered to notice me at all, it was to wonder if I'd last. I was still spending my school days on the sidelines.

That night Grandma could hardly get through her chores for her haste. The only hot water we had came from the reservoir in the black iron stove. We dipped water out to do the dishes in two pans on the kitchen table, one of suds, one to rinse. She washed, I dried, and she was rushing me.

"Grandma, where are we going?"

"To pay a call on Old Man Nyquist."

This town was full of people with one foot in the grave, if you asked me. "Grandma, is he real old?"

"Old as dirt," she said, "and deaf as an adder."

I sighed. "What am I supposed to say to him?"

"Nothin', if you're lucky," she replied.

So we were up to something.

Grandma and I were soon outdoors, bundled against the brisk night. I was pulling a little old red wagon from out of the cobhouse. You could find just about anything in the cobhouse. The wagon had been Dad's when he was a boy. Onward we went, kicking through the leaves. We might have been any grandma and her granddaughter, out for an evening stroll. But we weren't. We were Grandma Dowdel and me.

Old Man Nyquist was a farmer retired to town. He lived a street or two back from the Wabash tracks in a house on a corner lot. There was a barn behind. Not a light showed on his property. "He goes to bed with the chickens," Grandma remarked. But she looked hard at the house to make sure.

"What are we supposed to do, Grandma? Wake him up?"

"We're supposed not to."

Now we were in his big yard. Grandma looked up at a tree with a high canopy of foliage. She scanned the ground around it. "The old tightwad," she mumbled. "The old cheapskate." And she must have meant Old Man Nyquist.

"That's a pecan tree," she said. "Them's pecans." She pointed to the ground, but I couldn't see many. But then moonlight doesn't show everything, and a lot of leaves were down. "The old rapscallion said I could have any that had fallen. He knew there wasn't enough for a six-inch pie. I had an idea he was pulling my leg, the old . . ." But she was drawing out two gunnysacks from the folds of her coat, an old one of Grandpa Dowdel's. "Well, let's get what we can."

We bent double and worked the yard. "Be careful what you pick up," Grandma warned. "Not everything in a yard's a pecan. He keeps a dog."

It was dim, hard work. It took me forever to find a handful of pecans, and we were picking clean. Grandma was doing no better. She stood and ran a hand down her aching back. Her gaze fell on Old Man Nyquist's barn. A tractor stood just inside the open door. I guess he used it as a car after he retired to town. Grandma seemed to consider it.

She handed her gunnysack to me. Between us, we didn't have enough pecans for a tart. "If trouble breaks out," she muttered, "cut and run."

I stood rooted to the spot while Grandma drifted toward the barn, keeping the house in her sights.

The barn stood in its own shadow. Oil drums and chicken crates and bald tires leaned against it. Grandma stood in the moonlight. She rolled an old tractor tire off the heap. Hitching it under her arm, she advanced on the barn door. The nose of the old Massey-Ferguson tractor stuck out. She hung the tire from its radiator cap.

I was transfixed. I couldn't think a moment ahead. Now she was half swallowed by the darkness of the barn door. Then swallowed.

I stood like a sculpture in the yard. An ear-splitting explosion rocked the night. The tractor roared to life, coughing and gunning. Old Man Nyquist's dog shot out from under the porch, yelping, and chased himself all over the yard. The tractor lurched forward, gathering speed. As it crossed the moonlit yard, there was Grandma up in the tractor seat, white-headed and high. She could start it, but could she stop it?

The pecan tree stopped it.

Grandma, who didn't know how to drive an automobile, aimed at the tree and hit it dead on, ramming it with the tire over the radiator. The tree reeled in shock, and pecans rained. It was a good thing I wasn't standing under it. A ton of pecans fell together, like a hailstorm. When the tractor hit bark, it bounced back and the engine died. Grandma's head snapped back, but she was still riding it. Now she was climbing down.

She loomed up at me and reached for a gunnysack. "Grandma, did Old Man Nyquist sleep through *that?*"

31

"Who knows?" she said. "Work fast."

We were ankle-deep in pecans. "Like shootin' fish in a barrel," Grandma said. I scooped them up with one eye on the house. An old codger appearing on the porch with blood in his eye wouldn't have surprised me. "Keep at it," Grandma said. "He'd light a light first. We'd have a head start."

Finally I had so many pecans, I couldn't lift the sack. Somehow we got them into Dad's little red wagon. I was desperate to get away from there. Grandma had to hurry to keep up with me as I yanked the wagon around the corner and down the street. My heart thumped, and I wouldn't look back. Old Man Nyquist's dog was still yelping.

"Grandma, you didn't even put the tractor back in the barn."

"Didn't know how to get the thing in reverse," she said. "He'll just think it rolled out of the barn by accident."

With a tire hung on its radiator. "Grandma, that wasn't stealing, was it? I mean, in your opinion."

She was dumbfounded. "He *said* I could have any pecan that fell. And as long as we're out and about, we might just as well go ahead and get us some punkins."

"Oh, Grandma," I said. "Whose?"

They were the Pensingers' pumpkins. The Pensingers lived, like Grandma, in the last house on their street. We couldn't just seem to be strolling past, giving our pecans an airing. The street stopped in front of their house. From there on, it was just a cow path, and their pumpkin patch.

Only one upstairs window showed a light at the Pensingers'. I made a note to put a drop of oil on the wagon's squeaky wheels. When we came to their fence line, Grandma paused to take in the view. Behind us the town was like a little island of sighing trees and rising chimney smoke. Before us, the countryside unfolded, silvered by frost and moonlight. There the pumpkins lolled, gleaming beneath their scrubby foliage.

Grandma reached into Grandpa Dowdel's coat and drew forth the Halloweener's knife with the initials in the handle. The blade sprang out, and Grandma moved among the pumpkins. She cut free two nice big ones and another, medium-sized, while I stared unblinking at the light in the Pensingers' upstairs window. Grandma moved like a woman half her age, half her size. Somehow she balanced the pumpkins on the wagon among the pecans. I could just barely turn the wheels, but I longed for us to be somewhere else.

We were in sight of home when I said, "Grandma, in your opinion, was taking those pumpkins steal——"

"We'll leave a pie on their porch," she said. "And don't tip them pecans out of the wagon. We've already picked them up once."

We'd barely got everything into the kitchen before she was bustling. The frost was still on those pumpkins when she laid them open with the Halloweeners' hand-saw. She was soon spooning out the seeds and strings. She'd worn me out, but not herself. She popped the pumpkin parts, shells up, into the oven that never cooled. And all the while, she recited a little chant, under her breath:

> As much punkin as cream,
> Burnt sugar in a stream,
> Three big eggs, all beat up,
> And good corn syrup, 'bout half a cup.

She was almost dancing a hornpipe. To her, borrowed pumpkins were far sweeter than bought. Before she could tell me to start picking out the pecans, I stole away to bed.

But before the sun of that Saturday morning was up, we were baking. The kitchen was a heady heaven of vanilla and cloves and blackstrap molasses. Grandma sifted the Halloweeners' flour and worked it with salt and lard so I could roll out the pie crust. And she was particular about how I did it. I never had the rolling pin floured to her satisfaction. And I had to be reminded to roll the dough from the center out, and not back and forth. And exactly an eighth of an inch thick, or I had to start over.

I don't know how many pies we baked. And I don't know whose hens all those eggs had come out from under. But by nightfall we had a little red wagonload of the finest pecan pies and pumpkin pies you ever saw.

Grandma had no interest in going down to the school for the Halloween party, and said so. I looked forward to it because I expected we'd have the best refreshments of all.

"Are you wearing a costume?" Grandma inquired.

"Grandma, costumes are for little kids."

She hovered.

Then she decided to walk me to school for safety's sake. She was wearing her good apron with the rickrack. And I noticed the pheasant feather in her hat, which was dressy for her. I should have known that Grandma wouldn't dream of staying home from the party.

It was underway but limping when we got there. Carleen Lovejoy was at one end of the basement in a knot of her confederates. Gawky Gertrude Messerschmidt was one of them, and Mona Veech. Their idea of a party was to stand close and whisper. At the other end of the basement a grade-school teacher was trying to organize pin-the-tail-on-the-donkey for the little children, who were mostly ghosts and scarecrows. Between there were folding chairs for the grown-ups and old folks, under drooping twists of black and orange crepe paper.

Grandma filled the door, and people looked up in alarm and surprise. She was famous for keeping herself to herself, but she was everywhere at once, if you asked me. We parted the party like the Red Sea, bearing in our pies.

It was slim pickings on the refreshment table. A few popcorn balls, sticking to each other, two or three plates of fork cookies, a pan of fudge. The school board had provided a punch bowl of soft cider. Grandma cast her eyes over this bounty. "Good thing Effie Wilcox didn't bring her angel food cake," she observed, "or I'd have needed the handsaw to cut it."

She was shucking off Grandpa Dowdel's coat and turning back her sleeves. Of course she meant to serve up her pies herself. It was her moment of glory. We'd been working toward it all along.

Miss Butler appeared. She wore black sateen and a matching bow in her hair, which I personally thought was too perky for a teacher. "Why, Mrs. Dowdel," she said, "how . . . nice." Grandma wasn't exactly a member of the PTA. "And what delicious-looking pies."

"I'll need a stack of paper plates," Grandma said in reply.

Now people were lining up. Miss Butler found paper plates and throwaway forks, and two knives. Grandma and I began cutting up the pies. She could get more wedges out of a single pie than anyone I ever knew.

Mrs. Effie Wilcox was first in line. She was either Grandma's best friend or her worst enemy, depending on the day. And she was an unusual-looking lady. Cross-eyed, and her teeth came forth to meet you. "Well, Effie," Grandma said, "punkin or pecan?"

"Just a sliver of each," Mrs. Wilcox said, looking everywhere. "I'm cuttin' down."

I was shocked at how the grown-ups pushed in first. But then here came Ina-Rae Gage, who always looked so wan and drawn that I cut her an extra-wide slice of pecan.

When she was past, Grandma muttered to me, "That's the skinniest girl that ever I saw. She could rest in the shade of a clothesline."

Most of the kids from the high school jostled by. Milton Grider and Forrest Pugh, Jr., shied past Grandma. Carleen Lovejoy deigned to let me serve her, followed by her simpering group—Gertrude and Irene Stemple and Mona Veech. Our pie supply held out pretty well as half the town trooped past. Then I saw the principal, Mr. August Fluke, bringing up the rear.

When he came even with Grandma, we beheld a fearful sight. Slumping in front of Mr. Fluke was Augie, his son. Augie was in high school with us. But you wouldn't have known him. His head had been shaved and his scalp rubbed raw, beginning to scab. His bandaged nose was splayed all over his face. It was August Fluke, Jr., in a sorry state. Sullen too.

My jaw dropped. That skinned-up, bald head. That nose. . . .

I couldn't stand to look at him. Glancing down, I saw Grandma drop the knife she'd been using on the pies. She drew out of her apron pocket quite another knife, the one she'd found on the back walk by the privy. Somehow she managed to show the initials in its handle as she switched open the blade.

She plunged it into a pie and cut August Fluke, Jr., a slice with his own knife. Augie's eyes narrowed. Mr. Fluke spied his son's knife. Then his gaze traveled up to his son's shaved dome. How long, I wondered, had it taken all the Flukes to get the worst of the glue off Augie's head? That was glue that stuck till kingdom come.

Into Augie's peeling ear, Mr. Fluke barked, "Boy, you done took on the wrong privy."

Augie could see that Grandma meant to keep the knife. She looked past him to his dad, saying, "Punkin or pecan?"

To Grandma, Halloween wasn't so much trick-or-treat as it was vittles and vengeance. Though she'd have called it justice.

As she said later, we fed the multitudes. It was like the loaves and the fishes, with pie for all. After we'd been worked off our feet, one pie eater came back, nosing for a second piece. She was a big-boned, full-voiced lady. "Mrs. Dowdel, I declare that was the best pumpkin pie I ever put in my mouth."

Grandma could take compliments or leave them. "Who was that lady?" I asked her.

"Reba Pensinger," she said, sidelong.

Before the evening was over, we of the younger set, except for Augie, bobbed for apples. I brought home a couple, and Grandma and I baked them with brown sugar.

A Minute in
the Morning

I hated sleeping upstairs in that big square room at Grandma's. Joey wasn't across the hall like the summers when we were kids. The mattress on the big brass bed had more craters than the moon. And you could barely see your hand in front of your face.

In Chicago it never really got dark, not like this. And the house was too quiet, though things scuttled in the walls. Once in a while a thumping sound came from overhead in the attic. I didn't think Grandma's house was haunted. What ghost would dare? But she slept downstairs to spare herself the climb, so I was miles from anybody.

What I'd have done without my radio, I don't know. Grandma, who could hear all over the house, didn't like extra noise, so I played the Philco at night in bed, muffled in the covers.

With radio, you never knew. I could only pick up the Chicago stations if there wasn't a cloud in the sky, and it took a crisp, clear night to bring in KMOX from St. Louis. I didn't listen to much news. Most of it was bad. They still couldn't find Amelia Earhart, and ten million men were out of work. I knew my dad was one of them.

But I loved everything else on the radio. Baby Snooks. Fibber McGee and Molly. The A&P Gypsies. Edgar Bergen and Charlie McCarthy. Whispering Jack Smith.

The best thing about radio was that you couldn't see anything, so you pictured it in your mind. All the men were just as handsome as movie stars—as Tyrone Power. And all the women were as beautiful as you hoped you'd be. Their voices were who they were, and the biggest voice belonged to Kate Smith, the Songbird of the South. That fall the whole country was singing her "When the moon comes over the mountain, every beam brings a dream, dear, of you."

I'd lie there in the orange glow of the Philco dial, listening to the world. Then I'd see how fast I could fall asleep after I shut it off.

By November, I was cold. Wind howled in the eaves and found every chink in the house. With the window jammed shut, there was still a stiff breeze in the room, and I could see my breath. I took to wearing my old chenille bathrobe to bed over my pajamas. I considered wearing my plaid coat too, but thought I better save something back for winter. Finally, I made the mistake of complaining to Grandma.

You never saw a more surprised woman in your life. "Cold?" she said. "It doesn't get cold anymore. The climate's changed. When I was a girl, we had to walk in our sleep to keep from freezing to death."

One morning after a hard frost, Grandma stood at the foot of the stairs, banging a spoon against a pan, her wake-up call.

When I came into the kitchen, dressed in three layers, she was pouring batter on the waffle iron, and coffee perked. She let me drink coffee. The scent of her cooking breakfasts was to follow me through life. But I was sulky that morning.

"Grandma, what am I doing up at the crack of dawn? There's no school today."

She turned to give me one of her repertoire of surprised looks. It was daylight, and that was like noon to her. "Of course there's no school. It's Armistice Day."

People took Armistice Day seriously back then, nineteen years after the end of the Great War. In Chicago everything stopped at eleven o'clock, even the streetcars. People stood for a minute of silence, remembering.

"And the turkey shoot," Grandma said.

I knew they had a turkey shoot on Armistice Day down here. Posters were up in Moore's Store and Weidenbach's bank.

An awful thought struck me. A turkey shoot? What if Grandma took part? I remembered Grandpa Dowdel's old twelve-gauge double-barreled Winchester behind the woodbox.

Grandma read my mind. She was turning bacon and waved me away with the fork. "If I took out after an old turkey with that twelve-gauge, I'd blow him apart. There'd be nothin' left but wattle and shot."

The terrible picture of an exploding turkey raining feathers hung in my mind. But Grandma said, "It's not like that. They use air rifles and buy chances to shoot at paper cutouts. They don't shoot real turkeys. What would you do with a plugged turkey this far ahead of Thanksgiving?"

You could keep it upstairs in my bedroom where it would stay frozen. But I didn't say so.

"Besides, I don't compete." Grandma pursed her lips, ladylike except for the toothpick. "It's the men and the boys. You know how they love an excuse to make a clatter and show off."

A turkey shoot was bound to be outdoors, and my nose was just now thawing. "Then why are we going?" I asked, hopeless.

"For the burgoo," Grandma explained.

And I didn't even ask.

The Armistice Day turkey shoot was held on the Abernathy farm. Grandma and I went out there on shank's ponies, meaning we walked. They'd planted next year's wheat, and the autumn colors had faded. It was getting into the gray time of year. We tramped the road south, into the wind, until we saw horses tied to the fence posts and cars pulled off on the shoulder.

Grandma wore Grandpa Dowdel's old coat, and I wore his hunting jacket, and dungarees under a skirt. The longer I lived down here, the more I was starting to look like Mildred Burdick. A wool cap pulled down to my eyebrows didn't help.

The Abernathy farm looked long abandoned, though people milled around it. Out in a field they'd set up frames with orange paper targets more or less shaped like turkeys. And there was a gun rack. Since the turkey shoot was for charity, men in little caps were selling chances. They were the American Legion, veterans of the Great War.

The barn was in bad shape. And the house hadn't seen a lick of paint this century. All the ladies were clustered on the back porch.

"Does anybody live here?" I asked Grandma.

"Abernathys," she said, swinging wide the gate and marching up the walk. "That's Mrs. Abernathy in the door."

The other ladies clustered around a table on the porch beside a rusting cream separator. Mrs. Abernathy stood by, holding her elbows and looking down. She was a forlorn lady with a sweater pulled over her apron.

In the yard a big pot hung from a tripod over a crackling fire. It was the burgoo—a stew made with whatever you had on hand. White meat and red meat and maybe squirrel. Any old vegetable, heavy on the turnips. Potato wedges for body, stewed tomatoes for color, onions to taste. It was served at every outdoor event, from an auction to a hanging, as Grandma would say.

A small lady in a headscarf under an army cap stirred the burgoo with a wooden paddle. Grandma veered off the walk and took the paddle out of her hand. "I'll spell you, Wilma. Go for more kindling," she said, and the small lady fell back. The whole porch was watching.

I wanted to put some distance between me and Grandma, so I drifted out of the yard and down to the barn lot, where the crack and pop of air rifles rent the air.

Men and boys were ranked along the firing line before each distant turkey target. I didn't recognize any of them, but then they were all in caps with earflaps. They took their shooting seriously, but man and boy, they either weren't crack shots, or those paper turkeys were harder to hit than they looked. Both the barn and the shed were taking a pelting.

The American Legionnaires were handing over the rifles and reloading, and I must have been standing too close. A Legionnaire handed me a rifle, and I took it. At the touch of cold steel, I froze. From the way I was dressed, did he think I was a boy? Had he missed the skirt over my dungarees? This might have given Annie Oakley her big chance, but I was embarrassed to death. I couldn't wait to get rid of that rifle. I handed it off to the shooter next to me.

It was Augie Fluke, with his flaps down.

Ever since Grandma had glued his head, Augie had never looked me in the eye. He was a skulker by nature anyway. Now he blinked at the sight of me. But his eyes narrowed, and I read his mind. He was going to show me a thing or two about marksmanship. He knew my grandma was a dead shot, but she was a mere woman. Did I read all this in Augie's squint? If you're going to read minds, start with a simple one.

He jammed the butt of the rifle into one of his sloping shoulders. His tongue lolled out as he sighted down the barrel and took considered aim.

Then, as bad luck would have it, a scared rabbit, a big cottontail, darted from under the barn and across the front of the targets. Seeing live prey blurred Augie's judgment. Forgetting the paper target, he swung his rifle around to follow the rabbit. He swung too far. A big black car, a Buick, I think, was parked on the sideline. Just as the rabbit disappeared under it, Augie fired. The crowd looked at the car. In the silence you could hear a hiss as the back tire, a white sidewall, began to go flat.

A Legionnaire howled and threw his cap on the ground. He must have been the head Legionnaire, because the cap had medals pinned on it. "Dag nab it! That was a new tire! Who done that?"

Augie went rigid and thought about thrusting the rifle back into my hands. Then he flung it down and plunged headlong into the crowd. They made way for him, whooping and clapping and pretending to duck.

He vaulted a fence and hit the road running, back to town. So a turkey shoot wasn't as boring as I'd expected, quite. But I went on watching from up in the yard.

They shot some more. Then the head Legionnaire threw up his arm. "Troopers, hold your fire! It's pretty nearly eleven o'clock."

Silence fell. Some in the crowd took out their watches to make sure. It was the eleventh hour of the eleventh day of the eleventh month, the moment when the armistice of the Great War had been signed in 1918. We all turned to face east as people did, toward France.

I turned to see a back view of Grandma. Her left hand was outstretched, holding the paddle upright in the burgoo. Her right hand must have been over her heart. Her old hat was pulled low and pinned tight, and her hair was escaping. I never saw her shoulders straighter.

The ladies on the porch stood facing a blank wall because it was east. Mrs. Abernathy had turned in the door. An utter stillness measured a minute, with only the crying wind and the rattle of a dry creeper growing up the side of the Abernathy house.

Just then, did I see a face in a dormer window upstairs? I might have. I wasn't sure.

Then the head Legionnaire boomed out, "Gentlemen, lock and load!" The firing began again, like popping corn.

At lunchtime a bucket brigade of ladies in Legionnaire caps brought pails of burgoo from the pot to the porch. Now Grandma was up there, planted at the end of the table. Again, she'd pushed right in.

She threw back her coat. Underneath she wore an apron that was new to me. Though homemade, it was like the ones the hot dog sellers wore at Wrigley Field, with big square pockets in front to collect money.

Stomping in the cold, a crowd snaked up the porch steps. The Legion Auxiliary ladies handed over steaming tin mugs of burgoo. The line edged along until they came to Grandma. A mug of burgoo was a dime.

The first customer, a big old farmer, handed Grandma a coin. "I can't change a quarter," she said, dropping it into her pocket and looking straight through him.

"That's fifty cents for two," the next man said. "I'll take thirty cents in change."

"Haven't got it," Grandma replied, banking the fifty-cent piece. By now I was standing next to the porch just below her, bug-eyed to see what she was getting away with. Even I knew the next customer, Mr. L. J. Weidenbach, the banker. He was a big, sleek, slack-mouthed man as tight with money as Grandma herself.

He didn't wear a Legion cap. He may have been too old for the war. Anyway, he'd stayed home and made money. He held out a very thin dime.

Grandma looked at that dime like she'd never seen one. Her eyes were circles of astonishment. "That won't do it, L.J.," she said, loud. Mr. Weidenbach winced. The porch sagged with customers of his bank.

"What do you want from me, Mrs. Dowdel?" he muttered.

"From you I wouldn't say no to a five-dollar bill,"

Grandma said, louder than before. "If you can get the bootlace loose from around your wallet. The boys who fought at the front didn't count the cost."

The crowd behind him murmured. The Auxiliary ladies serving at the table stood tall and together. Their men had fought, many at the front.

The thought of five dollars for a cup of cooling burgoo made Mr. Weidenbach's eyes water. The line jostled him from behind, everybody all ears. He jammed two thorny fingers into his watch pocket and came up with a silver dollar, as high as he'd go. Grandma held wide her apron pocket for the banker to make his deposit. "Who's next?" she said as he stalked off the porch.

In short, she got more than a dime off everybody, except from those she knew couldn't pay more. In some cases she could make change, in others she couldn't. Once, I saw her palm the dime back into the hand that offered it.

A few people dropped out of the line when word reached them that Grandma was cashier. But it was burgoo or nothing. When the last customer settled up, Grandma had a pouch on her like a kangaroo.

Gloating was beneath her. But the toothpick in her mouth moved in a jaunty way, like a tiny baton conducting a small symphony. She helped herself to burgoo. When she noticed me, she handed me down a mug. It wasn't too bad, if you'd worked up an appetite.

Down the table, the Legion Auxiliary ladies drew into a knot, to confer. Then their leader advanced upon

Grandma. By the name on her cap, she was Mrs. W. T. Sheets. Her medals jangled importantly.

Grandma observed her approach. "Mrs. Dowdel," said Mrs. Sheets, "I'm here to tell you that you're twice as bald-faced and brazen and, yes, I have to say shameless as the rest of us girls put together. In the presence of these witnesses I'm on record for saying you outdo the most two-faced, two-fisted shortchanger, flimflam artist, and full-time extortionist anybody ever saw working this part of the country. And all I have to say is, God bless you for your good work."

With a small turn of hand, Grandma waved Mrs. Sheets away. Mrs. Sheets remained at her post. "Mrs. Dowdel," she went on, "you're not everybody's cup of tea. Well, it's common knowledge, isn't it? But we girls would be proud as Punch to have you join our Auxiliary if you're a veteran's wife. Did your late husband go to war?"

"Only with me," Grandma said, "and he lost every time."

I stood in the yard, clutching my tin mug. The knitted cap cut a groove in my forehead. My feet were blocks of ice. Grandpa Dowdel's hunting jacket smelled like dead ducks. But I'd never seen Grandma near this much money. I couldn't blink till I saw what she was going to do with it.

The Auxiliary ladies were collapsing the table and carrying their dirty mugs inside. Grandma followed them into the house, and I followed Grandma.

Mrs. Abernathy's kitchen made Grandma's look like

the Hall of Mirrors at the Palace of Versailles. The floor sloped. A pump stood over the sink and a coal oil lamp hung above the table.

Clanking loose change, Grandma looked on as the Auxiliary ladies went to work, dipping water out of the reservoir to wash the mugs. They poured the leftover burgoo into quart jars to leave with Mrs. Abernathy. They worked like beavers, drying the cups and boxing them up for next time. They wiped down the kitchen, leaving it cleaner than they'd found it.

All the while, Mrs. Abernathy stood in the corner, as if it wasn't her kitchen at all. She was so thin, you could almost see through her, and her eyes were vacant. She looked tired to death.

Then the other ladies were gone. It was just Grandma and me and ghostly Mrs. Abernathy in the dim kitchen. Something was about to happen, and I didn't know what.

In the flickering light Grandma spilled all the change onto the tabletop. It rolled and glittered. Grandma fished to find L. J. Weidenbach's silver dollar. She held it up in triumph.

Mrs. Abernathy stood at her elbow. The lamplight found all the hollows in her cheeks. At the sight of all that money, she brought her hands up to her face. "Oh mercy," she said in a husky voice. "In all the years before, it was never better than twelve dollars."

Grandma nodded knowingly. "Them Auxiliary gals mean well, but they're not enterprising. Burgoo for a dime." Grandma shrugged at the thought. Then, a little shyly, she said, "Will it see you through till next year?"

"It looks like riches to me," Mrs. Abernathy murmured. "And it'll have to see us through."

Grandma got busy. "We better bank all this money in coffee cans for safekeeping."

Mrs. Abernathy went for the cans. They scooped together, feeling all that metal money playing through their fingers, hearing its crash in the cans. "Shall we count it?" Grandma wondered.

"Oh, no," Mrs. Abernathy said, quick. "It'd scare me to know how much."

I thought I knew everything then. The veterans ran their turkey shoot to raise money for the American Legion. Their wives sold burgoo to help Mrs. Abernathy.

It was time to leave. She couldn't hide her coffee cans as long as we were there. But Grandma said, "How is he?"

Mrs. Abernathy looked aside, into the shadows. "He don't change much. Will you step up to see him? He won't know. But we don't get company, and it's quiet after the turkey shoot."

Mrs. Abernathy took notice of me for the first time. "I don't know if you want the girl to—"

"She can take it," Grandma said.

So I knew that whatever it was, I'd have to.

I followed behind them up the stairs, numb with not knowing. It was so low-ceilinged up there that Grandma had to duck. Mrs. Abernathy pushed open a door, and I smelled ointment and a sickroom.

It was under the slant of the roof. A wheelchair, an old-time one with three wheels and a wicker back, stood by the dormer window. He was sitting in it. Mrs. Abernathy's son.

She'd tied him into the chair with flannel strips, and his head was fallen back. His face was slick and raw, and his jaw hung open. He was far thinner than his mother, and his arms hung useless down the sides of the chair. When Mrs. Abernathy touched his shoulder, he turned toward her. Then you could tell he was blind. He turned his head away.

Nobody spoke. There was nothing to say. Grandma and Mrs. Abernathy stood together for a minute—a minute like the morning. Then we left.

We went in a hurry past the coffee cans on the kitchen table because Grandma didn't want thanks. Outside, I was surprised it was still daylight, surprised the world was still there.

The turkey shoot was over and the crowds gone. Down in the barn lot Mrs. W. T. Sheets sat in the big Buick, up on a jack. Mr. Sheets hunkered by the back fender. He was having trouble changing the wheel, and his spare looked low. The air was blue around him.

Grandma and I turned out of the gate and along the road, back to town. She set her mouth against the wind. It had turned, so we were walking into it again. And there was some winter in the wind. She tramped along, listening so intently to the quiet that I said, "Grandma, tell me."

"Her boy was gassed in the trenches," Grandma said. "And shot up."

We went on, the town rising on the horizon.

"He gets a check from the government, but it don't keep them."

"But, Grandma, aren't there veterans' hospitals where he could go?"

"She won't give him up," Grandma said. "She's lost him once already."

We walked a narrow stretch between the road and the ditch, single file. Then just above the sighing wind she said, "The trenches are all filled in, but the boys are still dying."

Then I could read her thoughts and I knew what this day meant. Mrs. Abernathy's son could have been my dad.

It was farther coming back than going. Counting fence posts made it longer. Finally we were in town, walking under bare branches. Grandma was putting the day behind her. You could see it in her stride. We turned at the business block, past Weidenbach's bank.

Something brought Grandma up short in front of Moore's Store. Under the turkey shoot posters was a display of Sweetheart soap. She stopped dead, though she made her own soap. Beside the display was a big picture of Kate Smith, the Songbird of the South, hand-colored.

She leaned out of the frame, smiling broadly. In her hand was a cake of soap. Below was her testimonial:

> *I start each day with a song in my heart,*
> *and a facial with Sweetheart soap.*

Grandma looked closer. "Looky there," she said. "That's Kate Smith. Do you suppose that's a good picture of her? I hadn't any idea she was such a big, full-figured woman."

Kate Smith was a very big, very full-figured woman. She was as big as—Grandma.

Grandma gazed at her picture with approval. Then on she walked with almost a spring in her step, though she was wearing boots.

By and by, I heard her humming. She wasn't a musical woman, so it took me a block and a half to recognize the tune. It was "When the moon comes over the mountain, every beam brings a dream, dear, of you."

Away in a Manger

Christmas was in the air, and Miss Butler had us girls making gifts in Home Ec. class. We ought to have been learning invisible mending and turning hems to make our clothes last. But Miss Butler decreed hot pads for our loved ones, made by crocheting used bottle caps into circular patterns.

Ina-Rae was my crocheting partner, and she was all thumbs with a crochet hook. Her hot pad bunched up in the middle like a skullcap. She wore it on her head until Miss Butler told her to take it off. I couldn't picture giving Grandma a hot pad made out of bottle caps crocheted together, so I let Ina-Rae have mine for her mother. I hadn't thought about giving Grandma any-thing. Somehow I didn't think Grandma and Christmas went together.

I was lucky to have Ina-Rae though. Carleen Lovejoy was still looking straight through me, and she set the tone for the rest of the girls. I hadn't made a lot of headway in all these weeks. Ina-Rae heard Gertrude Messer-schmidt tell Mona Veech that I wasn't as pushy as they thought I'd be. But that was as far as I'd got.

If there was one point in my favor, it was that I wasn't as well dressed as they'd feared. I had two wool skirts. One had been Mother's. The other belonged mostly to the moths. With my three sweaters, I could get through the week. But I was hurting for shoes, and my winter coat was a disgrace.

Carleen had five different outfits top to toe for every day in the week. She always wore silk stockings on Fridays, though some of her shoes may have been her mother's. Her sweater with drawstring neckline and pom-poms was much admired. But as Carleen said in her airy way, considering the boys in our school, there wasn't much point in looking your best.

But now Christmas was coming, and the annual school Christmas program, so we all had to pull to-gether. The entire student body was to be the chorus, though half of us couldn't carry a tune if it had handles. When Miss Butler ran us through "Angels We Have Heard on High," we sounded like starlings in a tree.

There was to be a Nativity scene, and she assigned us

parts. Joseph, the three kings, and some shepherds just about exhausted the supply of boys. Nobody wanted Augie Fluke on the stage. His hair was growing out, but he looked like a plucked chicken.

The girls' parts were for Baby Jesus' Mother and a heavenly host of angels. The idea that a boy could be an angel never occurred to Miss Butler.

The school was rocked by the news that I was to play Baby Jesus' Mother. I was surprised myself. Someone was heard to remark, "What was Miss Butler dreaming of? A *Chicago* girl playing the Virgin Mary. The idea!" It was Carleen. As we had to come up with our own costumes, I thought I could get by with bedsheets.

The program was all the Christmas some of us would have. Money was tighter than last year. The two topics on everybody's mind there at the end of 1937 were something to eat and money. Not that I ever went hungry at Grandma's. But there was hunger around. And with Grandma, money remained a mystery.

I made my way home from school one early December day, scooping snow with my open-toed shoes. Strangely, Grandma wasn't home. Just at dusk when I was up in my room, still wearing my old plaid coat, something drew me to the window.

Coming up the road by the Wabash tracks was a fearful figure. A lumbering, humped shape bent into the swirling snow. Its head was swathed in something. Strapped to its back was a long wicker basket. Its boots left black footprints behind. I hugged my skimpy coat tight and felt the empty house around me. The figure was at our fence line when it looked up at my window, and me.

It was Grandma.

I was down in the kitchen as she came in, shaggy with snow. She slung the big basket aside. Then she untied the shawl that held her hat on. She flung Grandpa Dowdel's old coat at a chair before the fire.

Underneath, she was wearing Grandpa's rubber chest-waders that were like rubber bib overalls. They strained across her bosom and pulled at the shoulder straps. She was all in black rubber almost up to her chins.

Of all the figures she ever cut, this one took the cake. I often wondered what she'd buried Grandpa Dowdel in. She seemed to wear every stitch he'd owned.

"Chilly out there." She rubbed her big red hands together. "My teeth is chattering like a woodpecker with palsy."

"Grandma, why were you out tramping the countryside in this weather?"

"First snow," she explained. "It's my busy season. It's all work, work, work. I'll die standing up like an old ox."

What good would it do me to question her more? I peered into the tall wicker basket. It was half full of shells—walnut hulls. They didn't tell me a thing.

I'll omit the scene of Grandma fighting her way out of all that rubber, beside the heat of the stove. It was like shedding a skin. Below it, she wore two crumpled housedresses and a cardigan sweater. Under that, a quick

58

peek of long-handled flannel underwear—a union suit, Grandpa's.

At the supper table I mentioned that Miss Butler had picked the parts for the Christmas program. I confided that I was Baby Jesus' Mother.

"They still doing Nativity scenes?" Grandma said. "We done them when I was a country girl in a one-room schoolhouse."

"What part did they give you?"

"Joseph," she said. "And once, a camel. I was always the biggest."

After I'd dried the dishes, I opened up my homework. They had homework down here too, sadly. Miss Butler could really dole it out. Mr. Herkimer was no slouch. Grandma sat at the other end of the table, nodding, while I tried to diagram some sentences.

I moved on to biology, falling into the rhythm of Grandma's snore. A Seth Thomas steeple clock stood on a high shelf. When it struck ten, Grandma jerked awake. She looked around the room astonished. It was her belief that she never slept, not even in bed.

"Is that the time?" She pointed down the table at me. "You better get booted and bundled up." She was out of the chair, shaking down the stove. Now she reached for her hat and the shawl and felt Grandpa's coat to see if it was dry.

I clutched my forehead. "Grandma, it's the dead of night."

"But a moonlit night." She shimmied into her chest-waders and stuffed her skirttails inside.

59

"Grandma, it's a school night. I need my sleep."

"Sleep? You'll sleep your life away and rot in the bed. You better pull on two pair of socks under your galoshes."

I had galoshes, but hated wearing them. "Grandma, where are we going?"

"After a character who's smarter than we are," she said, struggling into the coat, clenching her jaw.

When I came back to the kitchen, layered like Admiral Byrd, Grandma was rummaging through the mysterious wicker basket. She took inventory of various things buried in the walnut hulls. A coil of her picture wire. A handful of wooden stakes. She drew forth a small glass vial of some amber liquid. With a sly look my way, she uncorked it and passed it under my nose.

I reeled back. "Grandma, that smells nasty."

"Depends on who's doing the smelling." She rummaged on, coming up with what looked like a rabbit's foot. It was something furry off a rabbit.

"What's that for, Grandma? Good luck?"

"You might say so."

She stood to hoist the basket onto her shoulder. Then she remembered and made for a knife drawer in the Hoosier cabinet. Out of the drawer she drew a gun.

I froze.

It was nothing like the blunderbuss behind the woodbox. It was, in fact, a single-shot .22 pistol. But I didn't know that then. There was a lot I didn't know. Slipping the pistol into her pocket, she marched us both out the door, into the night.

We trod the icy ridges of the road, and the town fell back behind us. A cold, cloudless moon glared on white fields. I walked in Grandma's shadow, hearing the basket thump her back and the walnut hulls dance to her step. Of course, I should be sound asleep in bed by now, and I couldn't feel my toes. And Grandma was packing a pistol. But it was beautiful out here, like a black and white Christmas card. The ice on the woven-wire fences was a latticework of diamonds. And only Grandma and I were awake in all this stillness, at least I hoped so.

We must have walked halfway to Cowgills' farm before she nudged me off the road. We jammed a gate against a drift and entered someone's field. The snow was deeper here. Grandma led the way as we kept to the fences to the far corner of the field.

She put up a hand to hold me back. She wore rail-roaders' gloves. Then I heard the scream. A scream too human, from down in the dipping corner of the field that the moon missed. An answering scream froze in my throat.

Grandma shrugged out of the basket and whipped the pistol from her pocket. A moonbeam glanced the black metal of the narrow barrel as she aimed into the dark corner where two fences met. She fired straight into the scream. My knees begged to buckle.

She was down on all fours now, the black coat fanning out in the snow, her hands busy. She worked intently, biting off one glove to use her bare hand to do whatever she was doing. She tugged at a wire, and powdery snow shook loose off a fence post. Metal clicked. Then she pulled back and held him up, by the neck.

It was a fox—red, though black in the moonlight. His head lolled against her fist. His eyes were black beads. But he was dead, drilled through the head to put him out of his misery. A slender stem seemed to connect his hanging mouth to the snow. But that was a thin trickle of blood. I fought the supper in my throat.

Grandma dropped the fox in the snow and reached for the jawed spring trap that had caught it—a Victor #2, as I would come to know. She pulled herself to her feet to toss the trap into the basket. The walnut hulls were to disguise a human scent. So were the rubber chest-waders. Oh, I had lots to learn, once I was over the first shock.

Replacing her glove, she plunged her whole arm into the basket and came up with another trap. She fished for the tuft of rabbit fur and the vial of amber liquid and the picture wire.

Then she was down in the snow again, gasping with the work and the cold. Steam rose off her. She wired a trap to a fence post. She stuck the little flag of rabbit fur in the workings of the trap and drew the cork from the vial with her teeth. She'd driven the wooden stake. Now she poured a little of the fluid on it.

"Grandma, what is that stuff?"

"Fox urine," she said, and set the jaws of the trap.

Once more she dragged herself upright. We moved on along the fence. She gave me the trapping basket to carry, making me part of this. She swung the fox by his brush tail, after she'd reloaded the pistol.

"He's smart," Grandma said, mostly to herself but teaching me. "Wily. He can smell me, and I can't smell him. But there's some fox in me, and I know how he thinks. He likes fence lines and standing water and ditches. And I need the snow to track him."

We came to two more of her traps. I guess I was relieved to see them empty. Then on across another pasture a trap yielded a fox already dead. Though Grandma was quick on the trigger, I think she was glad of that. I was. She tied her two foxes together with twine from her pocket. She was never without twine.

We followed a fresh track of prints to the edge of a frozen drainage ditch where she set another trap. How quick and sure she worked with those stiff old hands of hers.

I was cold right through. We worked back to the road by a meandering route, leaving our own tracks behind. Now she had four foxes twined together. When she held them up, you could see how they'd be—fox furs with glass eyes, arranged around some lady's shoulders, far from here.

The next day Grandma skinned the foxes and nailed their pelts to the cobhouse wall. And when the fur broker came around, they did a deal. He tried his best, telling her he was mainly in the market for muskrat and beaver. But she was better with foxes, and at driving a bargain. She sold every last skin at her price. This began to clear up the mystery of where Grandma got such ready money as she had.

I went out with her many a December night when the snow was on the ground. Something drew me away from the warm stove. I dreaded the scream of a trapped fox. But I'd have heard it anyway, in my head, at home. So I'd go out with Grandma to work her traps in the ebony and silver nights. There were little changes stirring in me. I began to notice how old Grandma was, how hard she worked herself, how far from town she'd roam in the frozen nights, across uneven ground. I began to want to be there with her, to make sure she'd come safely home.

At school we practiced for the Christmas program all month long. Miss Butler couldn't sing either, but she was a feisty director. After we'd run "Lo, How a Rose" into the ground, she took it off the program. And she wasn't satisfied with our "Once in Royal David's City." She took the Christmas program personally, as teachers do.

We had our stage props now: a radiating tinfoil star and one of those mangers you see in Nativity scenes and nowhere else. Baby Jesus was a battered doll with eyes that opened and closed. It was Ina-Rae's. She said she'd had it when she was little, but the rumor was that she still played with it.

I had a sheet shawl and drapings. Carleen Lovejoy looked straight out of Hollywood in her satin gown and wings as head angel. But other people whined that they weren't nearly set for the big night. In a rehearsal both Johnson boys went bone-white and fainted. They had bad cases of stage fright, though they were only shepherds.

Grandma naturally took no interest, even when I complained to her about Carleen Lovejoy's halo. It was all tinsel and practically lit up. Grandma was busy. But then I wouldn't have taken her for a Christmas kind of woman anyway.

Still, one day after school I found her poring over mail-order catalogues. She handed me the one from Sears, open to "Fashions in Footgear for the Junior Miss and the Younger Active Woman."

"Pick you out a pair," she said.

"Grandma, do I get a Christmas present?" I said, to test her.

"You need shoes," she said. "Otherwise you'll be binding your feet in rags to get through the winter, like Valley Forge."

I considered every pair on every page, trying them on in my mind. A lot rode on my decision. These shoes had to go everywhere I went. And there'd be room in the toes, which made my heart sing.

Grandma had long grown restless when I finally made my choice. They had to be practical, with a closed toe. And still being fifteen, I wanted something a little older, with a Cuban heel. I knew they'd have to lace up, or Grandma wouldn't go for them. I checked off a pair—gunmetal gray to go with everything.

Grandma considered my choice. The toothpick hovered. "That them?" she said at last. "*Whoooeee,* two dollars and seventy-five cents." Her eyes filled her spectacles. "I remember when you could shoe a whole family and the horse for that money."

But then we drew paper patterns around my feet to send back for the right size. She filled out the order form with the toothpick aslant in the corner of her mouth. She stamped the return envelope. That's the only time I ever saw her use a stamp.

Later, I caught her studying the catalogue from Lane Bryant: "Winter and Spring of 1938 Modes for the Fuller-Figured Woman." But I stole away without a word.

The days slipped faster off the December calendar. Tension mounted at school, and both Johnson brothers were often absent. Carleen Lovejoy preened in advance. Clearly she thought that her angel was going to outshine my Virgin Mary. She was going to be the Christmas program's center of attention or know the reason why.

Something was coming over Grandma too. She was jumpier than a jackrabbit, and the short days were too long for her. One evening when it was hardly dark, she had us both out, tramping the road north. We pulled an old handmade sled of my dad's. "Grandma, now where are we going?"

"Greens," she replied.

When we came upon Asbury Chapel standing out in open country, I noticed the graveyard. It was screened by a stand of evergreens. "Grandma," I said. "You wouldn't."

No, she wouldn't swipe Christmas greens from a graveyard, though I heard it cross her mind. We tramped on to the timber in the bottoms along Salt Creek. There we found long-needled pine and blue spruce. Grandma took Augie Fluke's knife to them, and we began to stack the sled with greenery. Then, as if it was meant to be, we came upon a little fir tree. It wasn't three feet tall and far from full. But Grandma fell on it, and her knife gnawed away at its spindly trunk.

We trudged back to town with the greens tied to the sled. I went over the words to "Bring a Torch, Jeanette, Isabella" in my mind. Grandma was looking ahead.

By the night of the program, I should have known something was up. Grandma had lit the stove in the front room for the first time this winter. A merry fire crackled behind isinglass windows, and she was hanging a wreath in the bay. The Christmas tree stood in a nest of cotton batting on her marble-topped table. It was decorated with a string of popcorn and pinecones from the timber. On top was a tin star she'd cut out of a can.

I stood soaking in the warmth of the room, pine-scented. The idea of going to the Christmas program herself had clearly not crossed Grandma's mind. She certainly wasn't dressed for it.

I was. I had on my costume, bristling with pins. Under it my new gunmetal shoes, fresh from the box. And over all, last year's plaid coat. Now it had lush cuffs of red fox fur, making my sleeves long enough again. Grandma turned on me in surprise. She looked down to see I was wearing sheets.

"Grandma, it's the program tonight."

Waving away her own forgetfulness, she said, "Well, then, you better wear this." She produced something from a big apron pocket. It looked like a coil of baling wire.

She handed it over. It *was* a coil of baling wire. Twisted in it were tiny tin stars, cut from cans. A day's work to make. Grandma stood back, her hands clasped, a little eagerness in her eyes. "Watch out them stars don't dig your scalp."

She'd made me a halo so Carleen Lovejoy in all her tinsel wouldn't outshine me. It looked more like a crown of thorns, but I handled it, carefully.

I'd have come dangerously near kissing Grandma then, if she'd let me.

Then I was walking through town in galoshes to save my shoes. We'd done all our rehearsing at school. But the program was to be at the United Brethren Church. Though Jesus was born in a stable, the school basement didn't seem quite right.

The church threw stained-glass light out on the snow, and people flocked up the front steps. As I went inside, the train from St. Louis pulled in at the Wabash depot. The whole town became a little village under a Christmas tree, with the electric train circling and the glowing cardboard houses and the steepled church, sunk in cotton snow.

If you think one Christmas program is like another, you didn't see ours. The robing room where we girls got ready was full of bad omens. Who knew what went on across the chancel, where the boys were dressing in the choir room with Mr. Herkimer?

The girls who were only in the chorus flapped like bats in United Brethren choir robes. The angels were Irene Stemple, Mona Veech, Gertrude Messerschmidt, and the littlest angel was Ina-Rae Gage. None of their wings matched. Ina-Rae, the smallest, had the biggest wings—chicken wire. She could barely move in the room. It was like a birdcage in there. Then in swept Carleen Lovejoy.

Her shimmering gown, cut on the bias, was meant to outdo the other angels. Her halo hovered high over her head, supported from behind. She was made up for the New York stage. She'd shaved off her eyebrows and drawn on new ones. Her cheeks were pinker than nature. Her lips were a deep red Cupid's bow, with fingernails to match. She was a natural blonde, and that was the only natural thing about her.

Miss Butler edged into the room, and Carleen very nearly blinded her.

"Carleen! Wipe all that stuff off your face," she said, stricter than school. "You look like you're bleeding from the mouth."

Carleen bridled and stood firm. Seeing that I was in

three hanging sheets, Miss Butler turned to secure my costume. When I reached for my coat and drew out the baling-wire halo, she nearly swallowed her pins.

But there was an opening-night excitement even among us. From backstage you could hear the rustle of paper programs and the creak of pews. The organ boomed "Hark! The Herald Angels Sing!" and there was no going back.

The United Brethren preacher, Reverend Lutz, rose to quiet the crowd with a passage from Saint Luke. Miss Butler was pushing the choirgirls on. We in costume were to hang back here offstage, singing through the open door to add volume, but keeping out of sight until the Nativity scene. No choirboys came forth, because they were all in costume. But we could see shepherds and kings in the door behind Mr. Herkimer.

We sang our hearts out, onstage and backstage. Miss Butler kept the pacing peppy, though we never did get the bugs out of "Once In Royal David's City." Then came the tricky part.

We of the Nativity scene had to creep low under the curtains behind the choir. Here was the stable all set up, with cardboard sheep. I groped for my stool beside the manger. Above me Milton Grider fell into place as Joseph. We had shepherds behind us and kings opposite. Between, under the star, the heavenly host of so-called angels, Carleen at center stage.

From what I could see of Milton, he was wearing his father's bathrobe and a false beard. The kings were beginning to hold up frankincense and myrrh.

As the choir parted and broke into "O Holy Night," Mr. Herkimer pulled the curtain, and the lights went up on us. Mr. Fluke was the electrician. We'd practiced how to sit stone still for up to five minutes.

When we froze in place, I ought to have been looking into the manger at Baby Jesus. But the curtain caught me staring out at the audience, so I had to stay that way.

"Long lay the world in sin and error pining," sang the choir as I counted the house. The full pews gasped as we came into view, a living picture. And why not? Milton in bathrobe and false beard. Carleen like Sally Rand without her fans. Ina-Rae looking like she was about to take off. Me in baling wire and three sheets, showing a Cuban heel.

As I stared unblinking at the far door of the church, it opened. Grandma walked in. It had to be her. She filled the door. A tall man was with her. I watched her scoot people along a pew and sit. The pew popped like gunfire beneath her.

When the choir went into "What Child Is This?" the star lit up and sent a beam down on Ina-Rae's doll. This was to be the high moment, and was. The minute the beam hit the manger, Baby Jesus roared out a loud wail.

Milton moved. A shepherd's crook clattered to the floor. I couldn't hold my pose. I shifted my crowned head to see in the spotlit manger a real live baby, red as a beet, punching the air with tiny fists. Carleen was up-staged and went completely out of character.

A wave of wonderment swept the pews. Some people may have thought a living baby had been cast in the part. And if so, whose? But then Ina-Rae, flapping her wings, shrieked out, "Where is my dolly?"

Miss Butler fell back, and the choir broke ranks, never to reach "We Three Kings of Orient Are." Reverend Lutz, Principal Fluke, and Mr. Herkimer all advanced on the manger, like wise men in street clothes. But a newborn in a damp rag for a diaper, or swaddling clothes, stunned them.

Now people stood on pews, trying to see. Suddenly, Grandma was there, heaving up the steps past the pulpit. Her hat was alive with pheasant feathers. She reached into the manger for the red, squalling baby. She lifted it up, and the light was good.

The baby had one blue eye and one green. Grandma blinked. She held it up to the audience. "It's all right," she hollered out. "It's a Burdick!"

They talked about that Christmas program for years. In its way, it was the best one they ever had, though Miss Butler never really got over it. Of course the baby was another reason why Mildred Burdick never had been back after my first day of school in September.

Just when the Burdicks had managed to spirit an unwanted baby into the manger, we couldn't imagine. And why they thought the whole town wouldn't know another Burdick when they saw one, nobody could say. Grandma pointed out that the Burdicks weren't broke out with brains. The general view was that the United Brethren orphanage could find the baby a better home.

The evening lay in ruins on the stable straw at our feet. But there was one more miracle. I looked up at the tall man behind Grandma, and it was Joey.

Taller and leaner and handsomer. But Joey—changed and the same. And so I was looking my Christmas in the face. I hugged the wind out of him, tangled him in my sheets, nicked his chin with my halo.

It was Joey, fresh from the west, off the evening train. Grandma had sent him the ticket. That's where most of the fox money went. That's what it was for.

I had to turn away, quick. There was a lump in my throat, and that would mean tears on my face, and I didn't want Joey to see them. Then with a rush of wings, two angels lit on either side of me. The gawky one was Gertrude Messerschmidt. The dumpy one was Irene Stemple.

"Is that your *brother*, Mary Alice?" wondered Gertrude, suddenly my new best friend.

"Oh, Mary Alice, honey, he looks just like Tyrone Power," Irene breathed, feathering out. "But taller." Her pudgy small hand found mine in the drapings and she clung to me.

After we got home that night, Grandma showed me another ticket. It was a round-trip to Chicago for me, so I could go on with Joey to have some Christmas with Mother and Dad. It must have cost Grandma her last skin. First, though, we'd keep Christmas right here around the spindly tree in the warm front room. Just the three of us, like the old summer visits. Grandma and Joey and me.

But what I remember best about that evening is the three of us walking home from church. I see us yet, strolling the occasional sidewalks with our arms around Grandma, just to keep her from skidding, because she said she was like a hog on ice. And every star above us was a Christmas star.

Hearts and Flour

After several weeks of hard winter, this end
of the county is enjoying a January thaw. Mrs.
Dowdel, a lifelong resident, observes that "A
January fog will kill a hog."

    —"Newsy Notes from Our Communities"

    The *Piatt County Call*

We'd just finished up a Saturday breakfast when we
heard a pecking of sharp heels out on the back porch.
Grandma looked up. A shape showed in the steamy
window of the back door. There came a fumbled
knocking.

"Better let her in," Grandma said.

It was Mrs. L. J. Weidenbach, the banker's wife. Fools rush in, and she plunged past me into the kitchen.

Grandma looked her up and down. Mrs. Weidenbach's hat spilled black artificial cherries off the brim. Her upper arm clamped a big pocketbook, and her coat featured a stand-up muskrat collar. Grandma considered the fur with a professional eye. Her gaze fell to Mrs. Weidenbach's hemline, though she had to peer around the table to see. This may have been when Grandma saw that skirts were getting shorter.

Mrs. Weidenbach showed a good deal of leg. "I won't keep you, Mrs. Dowdel," she sang out, "as I see you are a busy woman."

Having polished off a plate of scrapple and corn syrup, Grandma lolled. "I will cut the cackle," Mrs. Weidenbach said, "and come straight to the point."

Mrs. Weidenbach never came straight to the point. Her voice dropped. "Word will have reached you about poor Mrs. Vottsmeier over at Bement."

"Will it?" Grandma said.

Mrs. Weidenbach clutched a chair back and leaned nearer. "The Change," she said.

"If she's thinkin' about making a change, who could blame her?" said Grandma. "Vottsmeier's no prize."

Mrs. Weidenbach rested her eyes. "I mean the Change of Life." She tried not to notice me nearby.

"Hitting her hard, is it?" Grandma inquired without interest.

Mrs. Weidenbach clutched her own furry bosom and

reeled. "The night sweats! The hot flashes! Of course it's nothing to what I suffered, but . . ."

Still, I wouldn't go away. I was just off her elbow, hearing every forbidden word. And she was coming to the best part. Her voice fell. "And her womb dropped."

"Do tell," Grandma said. "How far?"

"She says it *feels* like it hit the floor." Mrs. Weidenbach gave me a cold shoulder because I was sticking like Grandma's glue. "But as you know, I never gossip."

Grandma lurched in surprise. Coffee jumped out of her cup.

"All I am saying is Mrs. Vottsmeier is out of the running."

A dreadful vision of Mrs. Vottsmeier trying to run with some of her insides bouncing on the floor almost sent *me* reeling.

"And so we are up a gum stump about our Washington's Birthday tea. It's our sacred tradition to serve cherry tarts to honor General Washington. And as the world knows, there is nobody to touch Mrs. Vottsmeier for her cherry tarts." Mrs. Weidenbach's eyes snapped. "She is a plain woman, but there is poetry in her pastry."

"Who's throwing the party?" Grandma said.

"Who?" Mrs. Weidenbach blinked. "Why, the DAR, of course. The Daughters of the American Revolution, of which I have the honor to be president."

The DAR was a club of only the best ladies in town. They all traced their families back to the Revolutionary War (our side).

"As I expect you are aware," Mrs. Weidenbach said,

warming up, "my family descends from Captain Crow, who was at Yorktown when Cornwallis capitulated. My mother was a Crow, you know."

"Ah," Grandma muttered. "That explains it."

"Frankly, Mrs. Dowdel, one of the sorrows of my marriage is that I don't have a daughter and, yes, a granddaughter who will step into my DAR shoes when the time comes."

I couldn't help it. I looked down at her shoes. They were high-heeled and a size too small.

Mrs. Weidenbach looked at me bleakly. After all, she had no granddaughter, and Grandma had me. Now she began her retreat because the January thaw hadn't thawed Grandma.

"I leave you with this thought, Mrs. Dowdel. The Daughters of the American Revolution maintain a proud tradition of American aristocracy in even as humble a town as our own. Without cherry tarts, we are letting down General Washington. The town is still abuzz about your pumpkin and pecan pies. And I bow to nobody in my admiration for your flaky pastry. I charge you, Mrs. Dowdel, to play your part and come through for us."

With that, she was gone. We listened to her pecking off the porch. Silence fell like a benediction.

Grandma took her sweet time, then remarked, "Skimpy coat, wasn't it? She's courting pneumonia going around naked to the knee. She wasn't wearing enough to pad a crutch."

We sat at the table, listening to the icicles drip from the eaves.

Finally, I said, "Grandma, are we going to be making cherry tarts for her?" Because we'd need cornstarch, and we were about out of lard.

But she didn't hear me. "There's different kinds of people in the world," she said. "There's them who'll invite you to join their bunch. Then there's them who'll pay you for your work. Then there's Wilhelmina Weidenbach."

And that seemed to be her final word on the subject.

Winter resumes its grip as the younger set at the high school looks forward to an exchange of Valentine cards, and the DAR is abuzz about its annual Washington's Birthday tea.

　　The high school will have its big red hearts
　　But where will the DAR get its cherry tarts?
　　　　—"Newsy Notes from Our Communities"
　　　　　　The *Piatt County Call*

"What's all this about a valentine exchange?" Carleen Lovejoy said to Irene Stemple one February morning. "Nobody told me about it."

"Newsy Notes" may have been optimistic. There were a lot more girls than boys in school. And none of the boys seemed to be of a romantic nature.

Ina-Rae leaned over from her desk and pushed her big-eyed little face into mine. Somehow she still looked scrawny and incomplete without her wings. "It says in the paper there's going to be a valentine exchange," she whispered. "At the grade school we always made our valentines. We cut out hearts at our desks and put on lace. Elmo Leaper ate the paste. It was fun. Do you reckon we'll make them here?"

"I doubt it," I whispered back. "This is high school."

"Well, it beats what we're doing." Ina-Rae stuck out her tongue at her history book.

The classroom door opened. Principal Fluke stood there with a new boy. The day had been gray, but crisp winter sun broke through and seemed to find the newcomer. He was as tall as Mr. Fluke and lots better-looking. His hair was red-gold, according to the sun, and not cut at home. It was razor-trimmed over ears flat to his head. Forrest Pugh, Jr.'s, ears stood straight out, like open car doors.

"Miss Butler," Mr. Fluke said. "I got you a new scholar. Looks like my prayers is answered, and I got me a scoring center for my basketball team." Mr. Fluke pointed to the top of the boy's head.

Milton Grider flipped his pencil and slumped in his desk. At five nine, he'd been the tallest boy in school, till now. The new boy seemed to be six feet tall, easy. The back of Carleen Lovejoy's head vibrated.

"Name of Royce McNabb," Mr. Fluke said. "His paw's come in as surveyor for the county roads. Family's from down Coles County way. Mattoon. Let's call him a senior."

If Royce McNabb minded hearing his personal history blurted out in front of strangers, he didn't let on. But then, he was from Mattoon, which was citified for these parts. And sure enough, he was wearing corduroy pants, not overalls. An argyle pattern sweater strained across his broad shoulders.

Ahead of me, Carleen gripped herself. "Be still, my heart," she murmured loudly. Then she leaned across to Irene Stemple and said, "Hands off. He's mine."

"Move over, Milton," Miss Butler said, "and make Royce welcome."

Royce went through the day with the same smile for everybody. He'd probably been in a lot of schools and knew how to handle himself.

When I got home, I told Grandma we had a new boy at school. She waved him away. "The town's filling up with people you wouldn't know from Adam's off ox. Not like the old days when you knew your neighbors."

"The winters were colder back then too, weren't they, Grandma?"

"People starved to death because their jaws froze shut," she said. "You getting interested in boys?"

"Who, me?" I said.

At that, we heard Mrs. L. J. Weidenbach fumbling at the back door. When I let her in, there were ice crystals in her muskrat. She elbowed past me, her eyes teary with cold and emotion. Grandma had been over by the Hoosier cabinet. Now she was sitting down, seemingly at her ease.

"Mrs. Dowdel, we cannot pussyfoot anymore over these cherry tarts." Mrs. Weidenbach grappled with her giant purse and came up with the *Piatt County Call* newspaper. "I need a commitment. My land, it's in the paper now, where it has inspired two lines of bad verse."

Grandma didn't read the paper, so Mrs. Weidenbach shook it open and read,

> *The high school will have its big red hearts*
> *But where will the DAR get its cherry tarts?*

"Doesn't that turn your stomach?" she demanded. "I don't call it reporting, and I don't call it poetry. It's snooping, and possibly by a foreign power. The dignity of the DAR is on the line."

Grandma picked a loose thread from her apron front.

"Mrs. Dowdel, I need your answer before we get any more publicity of this sort."

"Oh well." Grandma turned over a large hand on oil-cloth. "If it's my patriotic duty, I'll bake up a mess of tarts."

The wind went out of Mrs. Weidenbach. She'd been geared up for a larger struggle, more on the lines of the Battle of Bunker Hill. "You will? Well, that's real . . . reasonable of you."

"All in a good cause," Grandma said.

Mrs. Weidenbach turned to go, but didn't make it to the door.

"On my terms," Grandma said.

Mrs. Weidenbach turned back, slowly.

"We'll have your DAR tea right here at my house."

"But—"

"It'll be handier for me," Grandma said. "I don't get out much anymore."

That was a whopper, but Mrs. Weidenbach's head was whirling.

"Mrs. Dowdel, let me explain. This is more than a social occasion. This is a meeting of our DAR chapter, strictly limited to our members. It is always at my house."

"I'll fire up the stove in my front room," Grandma said. "It'll be warm as toast in there."

"But—"

"Or you can serve store-bought cupcakes at your place."

Mrs. Weidenbach crumbled.

I was at school early on Valentine's Day, but Miss Butler was there before me. Since the newspaper had announced a valentine exchange, she thought she'd better fill in with a valentine of her own on everybody's desk. Hers were the flimsy kind that came in a sheet you punched out. So that was one valentine apiece.

When people straggled in, they found their valentines. "Honestly," Carleen Lovejoy said, rolling her eyes when she saw her valentine was from Miss Butler. She stuffed it into her desk.

Then here came Ina-Rae. On her desk beside mine

was Miss Butler's valentine—and three more. Ina-Rae clasped both hands over her mouth. She squeaked, and people turned to look. She was all eyes. And she really was the thinnest girl in the world. She was skinnier than a toothpick with termites. She looked around to see how many valentines everybody else got. One apiece.

Ina-Rae crept into her desk. Her hands dithered over the paper pile. She too made short work of Miss Butler's valentine. Then she took up the next one. It was home-made to a fault. It looked like it had been whittled, not cut out. The message read,

> I send this sentiment in haste
> But at least I didn't eat the paste
> A Secret Admiror

Ina-Rae stared, then leaned so far over, she was almost in my lap. "I think that one's from Elmo Leaper," she confided at the top of her voice. "Can you believe it?"

And, really, I couldn't.

Ina-Rae sat straighter in her desk now. Maturely, she took up the next valentine. It was somewhat better made, with odd little tufts of cotton batting stuck on.

It read,

> *Simple shepherds are we*
> *And too sheepish to say*
> *Have a happy St. Valentine's Day*
> *[unsigned]*

Ina-Rae gasped. Then she was all over me again. "The Johnson brothers? Can it be?"

As luck would have it, Elmo Leaper and the Johnson brothers were across the hall with Mr. Herkimer. But word that they'd sent Ina-Rae valentines swept our room like a grass fire. It didn't take long. There were only about twelve of us. Carleen Lovejoy looked back in annoyance.

Now Ina-Rae came to the last valentine, and I could hardly wait.

It really was lovely. A white satin heart, padded like a little pillow and surrounded by a double row of paper lace neatly pasted on—hours to make. Ina-Rae cradled it in trembling hands, to read,

To the sweetest little girl in this room,
or any room.

from R. McN.

"Oh, Mary Alice!" Ina-Rae bounced in her desk. She seemed overcome with self-confidence. Word radiated that Royce McNabb had sent Ina-Rae Gage a valentine.

Royce was there too, but seemed not to notice. He always brought an Edgar Rice Burroughs book, or a Rider Haggard to read before school took up. Word reached Carleen, though. Ina-Rae and I watched her vibrate.

Then she blew. Out of her desk, she switched and stalked back to us.

"Let me see that thing." She snatched the satin heart out of Ina-Rae's hands, ripping lace.

Carleen read the message for herself. Every word burned into her brain. She looked back at Royce Mc-Nabb. He sat there with his chin in his hand, reading. Royce was out of reach. Carleen slammed the valentine on Ina-Rae's desk, got down in her face, and howled, "What have you been up to, you trashy little squirt?"

A single tear replaced the gleam in Ina-Rae's eye.

Miss Butler came out of her chair. "Carleen! Leave the room."

So Carleen had to. Royce looked up as she slumped past him. The back of her neck was valentine-red and hot-looking. The door closed behind her. It was eight o'clock on the nose, so we all got up to give the Pledge of Allegiance.

Ina-Rae lifted her desktop to sneak peeks at her valentines all morning long, cooing loudly. Down in the basement at noon when we were eating out of our dinner buckets, all the girls wanted to sit near her, even Irene Stemple.

Royce shot baskets by himself down at the other end. He never really was a team player, though he had a nice hook shot. Not that I knew anything about basketball.

Carleen wasn't there. A smart mouth sent you home in those days.

Afterward, out at the pump, Ina-Rae sidled up to me. "That was fun. Did you see Carleen's face? I can keep the valentines, can't I? You sure dreamed up some swell messages, Mary Alice. Especially R. McN.'s. They must have took you absolutely days to make."

"All in a good cause," I said.

Ina-Rae had played her role well too. I'd liked the tear in her eye.

Then I went to scrubbing under the pump. My hands had been gummy for days. I thought I'd never get all the paste off them.

February turned out to be my busiest month. I was no sooner through making valentines than Grandma had me rolling out pastry for the tarts. And always from the center out. We spent the weekend before the DAR tea with towels around our middles and our hair tucked up. The kitchen was in a white fog of flour.

Then on Washington's Birthday, the tea was set for four o'clock, so I hightailed it home from school. In the kitchen the tarts were laid out on cookie sheets, little works of art, each and every one. Grandma was nowhere to be seen.

Then there she stood in the doorway to the front room. Grandma? She seemed to ponder the distance off my right ear. She was . . . posing. Her snow-white hair waved down from a neat center parting and drew back in a bun so tight, no hair escaped. Pearls hung in her ears. There were traces of Coty powder in the laps below her chins.

I'd never seen her dress. It must have been from the Lane Bryant catalogue. It was maroon wool crepe, with many a tuck taken across the prow. My gaze fell to her waist, where a self-belt was holding its own. And could it be? A lacy handkerchief was tucked up a cuff below one large wrist. New shoes peered out from below her skirts—fine big black patent-leather boats.

The tears started in my eyes. I wanted to hold her in that moment forever, framed by that door. "Grandma," I said, "you're beautiful."

She waved me away, but she was.

A flouncy white party apron she'd made for me hung over a kitchen chair. She tied it around my waist and pointed to a tray of punch cups. No tea appeared to be brewing, but she seemed to want me out of the kitchen while she made the punch. I carried the tray into the front room.

It was hot as August in there, and I nearly pitched all the glassware on the rug in surprise. A lady had already arrived and occupied the best chair. And she was no member of the DAR. It was Mrs. Effie Wilcox.

Mrs. Wilcox in a hat and an apron—but a nice, visiting apron. Her eyes and her teeth aimed all over the room.

Grandma had set up a table with a white cloth. I put the tray down. Turning, I had the next shock. In the rocker by the stove was another lady, wrapped in shawls and old as the hills. She wasn't DAR either. She looked like she might smoke a corncob pipe.

I couldn't tell if Mrs. Wilcox noticed me. You could never tell where she was looking. But the ancient lady was sound asleep because somebody had parked her too near the glowing stove. She was alive, though. You could have heard her breathing all over the house.

Back in the kitchen, I said, "Grandma, who's the old party on the other side of the stove?"

She turned from a large bowl of brilliant red punch. "That's Aunt Mae Griswold. The Cowgills brought her to town in their dairy wagon. She don't get out much anymore."

"Grandma, how old *is* she?"

"Oh, I don't know," Grandma said. "You'd have to cut off her head and count the rings in her neck."

But then a rapping on the front door echoed through the house. "That'll be the DAR." Grandma was cool as a cucumber, as if they often called.

When I opened the door, Mrs. Weidenbach swept in, followed by Mrs. Broshear, the undertaker's wife, and Mrs. Forrest Pugh. Then Mrs. Lutz, the preacher's wife, and last, Mrs. Earl T. Askew. All of them were hatted and corseted, veiled and gloved. They sensed trouble at once.

"Oh, tell me I'm wrong," one of them blurted. "Is that Effie Wilcox?"

"Howdy," Mrs. Wilcox said, looking them all over at once.

They spotted Aunt Mae Griswold. Her jaw had dropped. She had two teeth, and she whistled as she snored. They stared. "She'll be next," said the undertaker's wife.

Then they looked up to see Grandma, tall in the room, her big fingers laced before her. She looked as good as any of them. Better, if you ask me. They knew at once she was in charge of the party.

"You can throw back your coats," she said in welcome, "or this girl here will take them."

Mrs. Earl T. Askew was in Persian lamb and wouldn't give me her coat. She longed to flee. They milled in the room, running into each other. Nobody wanted to sit next to Mrs. Wilcox. They noticed the pink silk pillow with the gold fringe Grandma had put out to dress up the sofa. It bore the message,

SOUVENIR OF STARVED ROCK, ILLINOIS

I brought out kitchen chairs. Mrs. L. J. Weidenbach called the meeting to order, though she was rattled. "We will dispense with our usual order of business," she began, "as we are not . . . alone. But I will call upon Mrs. Lutz to give the invocation."

"How about a swig of fruit punch to wet your whistles first?" boomed Grandma.

I went to the kitchen for the punch bowl and handed around brimming cups. Mrs. Lutz rose for the invocation, which went on and on. I had time to bring out all the refreshments. When Mrs. Lutz finally ran down, Aunt Mae Griswold came to sudden life. "Amen, sister!" she called out, waking in a crowd. She may have thought she was in church.

"Who are you, honey?" Aunt Mae inquired of Mrs. Weidenbach, who sat too near her.

"We are the DAR," Mrs. Weidenbach said, sniffy. "We trace our families back to the American Revolution."

"Speak right up to her," Grandma roared from the kitchen door. "She's deaf as a post."

"Speak right up to me," Aunt Mae said. "I'm deaf as a post. But I'm talkin' about you, honey. Who was you?"

"I was Wilhelmina Roach before my marriage." Mrs. Weidenbach spoke stiffly, but she was willing to give her history. "I trace back through my mother to the Crows of Culpeper County, Virginia, and Captain—"

"Oh, honey, you don't." Aunt Mae was wide awake now. Bright as a button. The room hung suspended. They hardly noticed when I refilled their punch cups.

"You'd be about, what? Fifty-six?" Aunt Mae squinted. Mrs. Weidenbach paled, and took a quick swallow of punch.

"I well remember when the Roaches took you," Aunt Mae recalled. "It was about 1883, wasn't it? You was a Burdick."

All the air went out of the room.

"The county took you and your sister away from the Burdicks, as they was all mostly in the pokey at that time. You and your sister was put in separate foster homes. Nobody wanted both of you. I remember it like it was yesterday." Aunt Mae sat back and rocked. "Oh yes, you're a Burdick. That green-eye, blue-eye trait come into the family later from a lightning-rod salesman."

The silence was deathly.

Mrs. Effie Wilcox rose from her chair. Her hat hung from a single pin. "And the Schultzes took me!" she cried out. "They never wanted to tell me who I was. They said it would mark me for life!"

The DAR ladies fell back. Mrs. Wilcox made a bee-line across the room. "You's my long-lost sister!" She flung out her arms to Mrs. Weidenbach, who flinched. Punch went everywhere, and horror and defeat were written in her face.

The afternoon descended from there. Mrs. Askew fled, perhaps to spread the news. The rest circled Mrs. Weidenbach to support her and wall out Mrs. Effie Wilcox. The front room was as hot as the Amazon jungle, and several needed a third cup of punch.

They were in tears now, and Mrs. Weidenbach was hysterical. They bore her away, out the front door in a gaggle, their hats over their ears and their veils trailing.

None of them walked a straight line, and Mrs. Wilcox wove after them in pursuit. And come to think of it, she and Mrs. Weidenbach had the same coloring. Pasty-faced. Different teeth, but Mrs. Weidenbach's may not have been her own. Mrs. Wilcox paused at the front door where Grandma was seeing her guests off. "I guess Wilhelmina is broke down with joy at finding me at last," Mrs. Wilcox said.

"Very likely," said Grandma, closing the door behind

them all. She turned to savor the quiet of the room. Aunt Mae Griswold had dropped off again. Her jaw gaped. She snored a little whistling, sleepy-time tune.

Grandma spoke low. "What in Sam Hill are we going to do with all them tarts?"

But we got through them in time. There wasn't a drop of punch left. It had been one part strawberry juice and two parts Kentucky straight bourbon. I found the empty bottle of Old Turkey later.

In a sharp break with tradition, Mrs. Dowdel was hostess for this year's DAR Washington's Birthday tea. Honored guests were Mrs. Effie Wilcox and Aunt Mae Griswold.

A sudden cold snap has cost the life of a heifer on the Bowman farm and killed a hog.
—"Newsy Notes from Our Communities"
The *Piatt County Call*

I wrote out my latest "Newsy Note" and copied it over neatly. As Miss Butler always said, the only *real* writing is *re*writing. Then I dropped it off as usual down at the post office on my way to school.

A Dangerous Man

Spring and I stirred. For my sixteenth birthday present in March, Mother sent me a dollar, all folded up. I don't know where she got it.

The farmers planted alfalfa on the day after the new moon. The oats and clover went in. Now in April they'd planted corn in the field next to Grandma's house. The sap was rising, and the seasons turned like a wheel.

I hadn't seen much of Bootsie all winter long. She didn't turn up for her treat on the back porch anymore. She was finding her own suppers. Once in a while I'd see her shadow against the snow. She was going about her business, being a country cat.

Then in the spring when you could smell the ground, Bootsie turned up. She found a way to climb the house—up the front porch trellis, I guess. She did her high-wire act along a slanting drainpipe, all the way to my window. I never knew how she did it, though she could see in the dark.

I'd let her in, of course, and Grandma knew.

Bootsie would drop in off the windowsill. If she felt like it, she'd jump on my bed. I'd make a tent of the covers, and sometimes she'd take a chance and climb inside, eyes aglow like the dial on the Philco. She'd claw a nest and curl up in the crook of my arm like the old days. She was more of an armful now, and she smelled like the cobhouse.

But Bootsie never lingered. Some nights she'd hear that faint thumping sound from the attic, and she didn't like it. She'd fight out of the covers, glare at the ceiling, and be gone.

I'd ruled out ghosts, so I was used to that sound from above. Weeks went by without it. But I'd wake in the night, and it had been the thump from up there. Once, a bird cried out and suddenly stopped, in the middle of the night.

By April Bootsie took time out from her busy schedule to bring me offerings. One afternoon I found a robin's egg on my bed. Had the robin flown in the open window and laid it? But no, Bootsie must have carried it in her mouth all the way up the house for me. I was touched.

The next one was a dried-up grasshopper. Then a field mouse, dead as a doornail. Then part of a frog, very ripe.

One day when I came in, the present on my bed moved. Mewed. It was a kitten, a miniature Bootsie with bird-brittle bones and four white paws in the air. I named her April on the spot. She was so tiny and breakable, I was afraid to touch her. But I meant to keep her. She'd replace Bootsie. I'd get a box of sand up here for her and sneak food from—

But then Bootsie appeared on the windowsill. Dropping down, she gave the ceiling a quick, cautious look. She leaped on the bed, snatched up her kitten by the scruff of the neck, and was out the window before you knew it.

Bootsie had only brought her for a visit, to show me. Now she was taking her baby back to the cobhouse where they lived. So that's the way it worked. I stood in the afternoon light and shed a tear or two. It didn't take much to set me off, now that I was sixteen.

That Saturday was summer-warm. "Bring down your sheets," Grandma hollered up the stairs at the crack of dawn.

She liked to boil her laundry in a big pot over an open fire in the yard. She didn't have a wringer, so we wrung out the sheets by hand. It was like tug-of-war once she dug her heels in. By the time we hung them on the line, they were half dry and we were wet through.

By noon the day was so hot that we decided to wash

our hair and sun-dry it. We used rain-barrel water and her homemade lye soap. I can still feel her knuckles in my scalp, and that lye soap took forever to rinse out. I hadn't had a finger wave since last summer. Grandma had been cutting my hair.

She pulled out her pins and combs to let down her hair, and that was a bigger job. Her hair fell to her waist. She bent into an enamel pan on an old pine table in the yard, and I lathered her head.

"Dig in," she said. "Get them cooties where they live." But she had an awful lot of hair. We rinsed in cold water, and she came up gasping time after time.

She wrung out her hair in the sun. It was whiter than the clouds scudding overhead. Oh, that bright afternoon, scented with lye and the greening earth. And Grandma shaking out enough white hair to nest a flock of birds.

A spanking breeze had dried the sheets. I was taking them down when a man started across the side yard. A stranger. "Grandma," I said, to warn her.

"Whoa," she called out to him. "What's your business?"

He carried nothing in his hands and looked travel-worn. I wondered if he was a drifter who'd wandered away from the Wabash tracks.

"I'm looking for a room," he said in a funny accent. He was a little fellow for this part of the country.

"Who sent you to me?"

You can picture how Grandma appeared to him. He looked up to see all that hair standing out around her head like a mane. Her skirts were hiked to keep out of the laundry fire. Each one of her legs was as big around as his waist.

"The postmistress," he said, blinking through horn-rimmed glasses.

Grandma looked skeptical. "Maxine Patch sent you to me?"

I knew Maxine Patch, the postmistress. When I was still sending my "Newsy Notes" to the county seat newspaper, I'd had to deal with her. I'd given up writing "Newsy Notes" before people found out who was writing them. I was learning from Grandma how to keep my business private.

"She just said I'd have to go door-to-door to see if anybody'd rent me a room." The stranger still stared. Grandma was such an awesome sight that he could hardly keep his thoughts in order. "And you're the last house in town. Don't you people have a hotel around here?"

"Used to, but it was burned to the ground in the War of 1812." Grandma watched him to see if he was dumb enough to believe the War of 1812 had been fought around here.

He was.

"Where you from?" she asked.

"New York."

He stood drooping in the yard, keeping his distance from Grandma. "I'm here from the WPA. The Works Progress Administration."

"The government?" Grandma's eyes narrowed.

He nodded. "I'm supposed to do some painting in the post office."

"Give it two coats," Grandma advised. "The paint's about the only thing that's holding it up." The post office was a one-room shanty behind The Coffee Pot Cafe. It used to be the barber shop.

"Not that kind of painting," he said, tired. "I'm an artist. I work large. Murals, mostly."

Now Grandma stared. But I knew what he meant. The federal government had sent WPA artists to Chicago to paint murals in public buildings up there. The lobbies were painted over with big tough women and bulging men in workshirts, swinging hammers and sickles, all of them larger than life.

So was Grandma, as the stranger could see. "Well, you won't get a mural on our post office," she told him. "There's not room in that crackerbox to hang up your tintype."

He knew that. "But they cut my orders in Washington."

Now Grandma's eyes narrowed to slits. "That's our tax dollars in action," she said. "What they paying you?"

"Four dollars per diem," he said.

"Son, you're home," Grandma said. "It ought to take you about a month not to paint a mural in the post office. I charge two dollars and fifty cents a day. You can get your meals up at The Coffee Pot Cafe."

I nearly keeled over. I didn't think the Palmer House

Hotel in Chicago charged two dollars and fifty cents for a room. But Grandma judged it was fair. She saw a chance to recover some of her tax money from the government. Though I doubted if she paid taxes.

"It's steep rent," the stranger said, bravely.

"And the last house in town," Grandma replied.

That's how we got our lodger, Arnold Green, the New York artist. Grandma shook him down for ten dollars in advance. She sent me inside for some of Grandpa Dowdel's clothes. And she aimed him at the cobhouse to skin off what he was wearing. She built up the fire and tossed his traveling clothes into the pot. She threw out his socks and scrubbed his shirt on the washboard, white hair flying.

"Laundry included in the rent," she said generously.

Grandma gave Arnold Green the bedroom facing the Wabash tracks. In its closet was the trapdoor to the attic. She provided a ladder so he could use the attic for an artist's studio. She was generous to a fault. He collected his easel from the depot and set it up under the attic's slanting rafters.

I couldn't sleep upstairs next door to a man. I had to sleep downstairs on a cot at the foot of Grandma's bed. And she could outsnore Aunt Mae Griswold, but the money was rolling in, so what could I say?

Word went out like the wind that Grandma had snagged an artist on government pay and was charging three, four, as much as five dollars a day, depending on who told it.

Arnold Green was no trouble. He came and went and lurked in the attic most of the time. He was such a small man, you hardly noticed him.

Not that Grandma didn't take an interest. One night when he was passing through the kitchen on his way up to The Coffee Pot Cafe, she stopped him cold in the door. Though she never pried, she said, "You a married man?"

He said he wasn't.

"You thinking about getting married and settling down in these parts?"

He staggered back from the screen door and turned. "In *these* parts?" He looked horrified. His hair nearly stood on end.

"Why not? It's a better climate than New York," said Grandma, who'd never been there. "It's the healthiest spot in Illinois. We had to hang a man to start the grave-yard."

Arnold Green bolted into the night.

We sat on at the kitchen table, over the remains of supper. "Grandma, were you pulling his leg?"

"I was giving him fair warning," she said. "Maxine Patch found him on the first day. She'll be up at The Coffee Pot this minute, layin' in wait. She's thirty-six and man-hungry." Grandma's lips pleated knowingly, and the toothpick pointed out this truth. "And there hasn't been an unmarried man around here since the last chain gang went through."

I didn't know what to make of that. Maxine Patch had a figure you noticed, but not the face to go with it.

And she was thirty-six, so I probably thought that was way too old to be thinking about romance.

Besides, I had other matters on my mind. Personal business. Final exams were coming up, and I wasn't pulling my weight in Mr. Herkimer's math class. First semester, I'd collected a C, happy to get it. Now I didn't know if I was doing that well. It was business math this spring, full of percentages, dry measures, and profit-and-loss. I couldn't make head or tail out of it.

Royce McNabb was a math whiz. One of the rumors swirling around him was that he was teaching himself trigonometry, whatever that is. And he was the best-looking boy in the county. So I formed a plan. I'd been forming it since Valentine's Day, but now I'd have to speak to Grandma. Catching her in a quiet moment, I said, "I'm falling a little behind in math."

She listened, narrow-eyed.

"I thought I'd ask that new boy to come over. Royce McNabb, I think his name is. So we could study together."

"Do tell." Grandma pondered. "Think he knows more math than the teacher?"

Well, no, but—then I saw she was pulling my leg. I thought I'd better come clean, never an easy decision at sixteen. "Grandma, Carleen Lovejoy's set her cap for him. And I want to make my move before she makes hers."

That was talking her language. "We'll squeeze some lemons for a pitcher of lemonade," she said.

But that didn't solve everything. I wanted to invite Royce on Sunday afternoon because that was when Grandma napped. The whole town did.

"We could study in the front room where it's quiet," I said to her carefully.

She gazed upon me like the sphinx.

"Grandma, I want you to leave us alone. You know how people talk about you. How you're trigger-happy and things like that. I don't want you scaring Royce off."

"Who, me?" she said, the image of astonishment.

Then I had to get up the nerve to invite Royce, and we'd scarcely spoken two words to each other. And I couldn't just barge up to him. Carleen watched him like a hawk all day long, and I didn't want to show my hand. Finally, I wrote him a note. I was better in composition than math. I slipped it to him, and he slipped it back. Written on the note in his square hand was,

**OK,
Royce**

I still have it.

As Grandma would say, that Sunday afternoon liked to never come. I counted the hours and nearly wore out both my summer dresses, trying them on to decide which to wear. Now I don't remember which I chose.

When Sunday afternoon finally came, the whole town

was sleeping off big dinners as I paced the front room. Grandma was offstage but audible. I could hear her two rooms away. One of her snores had a whistle in it like Aunt Mae's. Her other one was low and throaty, like pigs eating clinkers.

A pitcher of lemonade stood on the marble-topped table. I was sweating more than it was. For some reason, I thought it would look nice if I was carrying a lacy handkerchief when Royce got there.

I heard the kickstand on his bike ring on the concrete of the front walk. I'd unlatched the screen door so I could sweep it open to him without a fumble. It seemed to me I'd thought everything out.

When Royce filled the door, I thought of Joey. Royce was that tall, that broad across the shoulders. Then I fumbled the doorknob because my lacy handkerchief was a damp ball in my hand. I'd ripped it in two. And I wished I'd had some perfume to wear, just a dab behind each ear, in case that worked on a boy.

Somehow I got Royce inside. We stood there, alone at last. I was lightly scented with lye soap. His red-gold, sunstruck hair was tousled from his bike ride. I stood near enough to have to look up to him.

He looked down and spoke to me, really for the first time. "You know," he said in his manly voice, "percentages are basically decimals. Maybe we ought to start there."

I blinked. Did he notice I didn't put that stuff on my eyelashes that Carleen put on hers? And no, we weren't going to start the afternoon with decimals. That could lead to fractions. I drew Royce across the airless room to the lemonade.

We sat there with glasses in our hands, listening to Grandma snore.

"My grandmother," I explained, with a little shrug and a shy smile I'd never used before.

"That'd be Mrs. Dowdel?" Royce looked curious, wary.

I nodded, looking aside. Butter wouldn't have melted in my mouth.

Royce sat with legs apart, elbows on knees. Actually, he sat like Grandma did. Then he said, "We have something in common, you and me."

"We do?" Oh, how close to simpering I was. Another minute and you wouldn't know me from Carleen.

"I'm a stranger here myself," Royce said. "I'm from Mattoon. You're from Chicago. We're a couple of foreigners here."

Royce McNabb was finding things we had in common, without even being prompted. Sweet, silent Sunday afternoon seemed to unfold before us, and I could swear I heard violin music from nowhere. I searched for a reply worthy of Royce. I searched too long.

A bloodcurdling scream from over our heads cut Sunday afternoon in two.

Then mingled screams, from up in the attic, and crashing and banging like you never heard. Royce came up in a crouch.

105

We both heard Grandma's feet hit the floor by her bed. When she galloped into the front room, she was wearing an old bathrobe and Grandpa Dowdel's Romeo house shoes. Her spectacles hung from one ear. On her way through the kitchen she'd grabbed up her twelve-gauge Winchester from behind the woodbox.

"Where's it coming from?" she demanded.

Royce shied at the sight of the gun, and Grandma, but we both pointed to the ceiling. Plaster dust sifted down. Now the crashing and banging and running into things was coming from straight overhead, from Arnold Green's room.

"Hoo-boy," Grandma said.

When Royce could tear his eyes off Grandma in sleep-wear, heavily armed, he knocked back his lemonade. The noise from above was still terrific, like the ceiling could give way any second now. But Royce looked ready for anything, except what happened next.

Somebody was thundering down the stairs. When she came into view, it was Maxine Patch, the postmistress. Draped and coiled all over her was the biggest snake I've ever seen outside the Brookfield Zoo.

Maxine was screaming for her life, and that snake was all over her. It looped around her shoulders where it seemed to have dropped on her. It clung to one of her sizable hips. And there was still snake to spare.

And though I couldn't believe my eyes—and heaven knows, Royce couldn't believe his—the snake was all that Maxine wore.

She did a dance around the platform rocker, bare-foot. Bare everything except for a rose in her hair. She was all ghastly pale flesh and black snake. And she couldn't shake that snake for all the shimmying in the world.

Grandma worked around her to get the front door open. With a scream and a hiss, Maxine and the snake leaped through it. They did a fast Hawaiian hula off the porch and skimmed around the snowball bushes, making for town.

"That's too good a show to keep to ourselves," Grandma said.

With the thought, she was through the door and out in the front yard. Planting her house shoes, she jammed the Winchester into her shoulder, aimed high, and squeezed off both barrels. The world exploded. Birds rose shrieking from the trees, and the town woke with a start.

Royce and I watched from the door. I was half dead with embarrassment. Royce rubbed the back of his neck in a dazed way, but he was all eyes when it came to Maxine's retreating figure. We saw the snake drop off her just as she left our property.

But Maxine kept going, racing for the post office. She lived with her folks, the Ivan Patches, but she couldn't go home wearing only a rose. Did she think she could make it all the way to the post office unnoticed? If she'd been thinking at all, she'd have doubled back to brave Grandma and get her clothes. But she didn't. When people alerted by the gunfire ran to their windows, they saw Maxine Patch as nature intended, speeding past their houses and straight into the annals of undying fame.

Grandma dragged the shotgun back to the porch pillar. There she sagged and seemed to weep, in mirth or joy. Then she came on back inside, pushing past Royce, who seemed turned to stone, though he was never a big talker.

"*Grandma,* what in the world was a snake that big doing in the house?" I said, at the end of my rope. "What was *any* snake doing in here?"

She propped the smoking gun against the marble-topped table to wipe her wet eyes. She hooked her spectacles over both ears. "That snake lives here, up in the attic."

So that was what had been thumping right over my room all this time. A hideous, huge, coiling, striking snake directly over my head. Bootsie knew.

"Grandma, *why?*"

"It keeps down the birds," Royce said, recovering.

"That's right," Grandma said. "Birds get in under the roof of an old house. You can't keep them out. But a snake will keep them down."

Royce was edging around her, to the door. "Well, I probably ought to get going," he said. "But . . . thanks. It was a real interesting afternoon. I never saw a—" But now he was gone, pedaling away down the walk. And all my hopes went with him.

I turned on Grandma. But then we both saw Arnold Green standing there, swaying at the foot of the stairs. He was gray-faced, ashen-lipped. His eyes stared out of his horn-rims. He was a wreck in an artist's smock. A brush was frozen in his hand. He tried to speak.

Grandma observed him severely.

Still in shock, Arnold Green said, "Sh—sh—sh—"

"She's gone," Grandma said. "The snake peeled off, but Maxine kept travelin'."

"It fe—fe—fe—"

"Fell on her in the attic. It lives in the rafters," Grandma said. "I forgot to mention that."

Arnold Green said, "It's been up there a—a—a—"

"All along," Grandma said. "And I don't allow women upstairs."

"She was po—po—po—"

"Posing?" Grandma said. "Well, I better make a rule against painting pictures of naked women in my attic."

"Not na—na—naked. *Nude*," said Arnold Green. "I studied in Paris."

Grandma didn't throw him out and send him on his way. Not at two dollars and fifty cents a day. Arnold Green brought his easel down from the attic that same Sunday afternoon. Something Grandma said left him with the impression that the snake was gone for good. Still, he nailed the trapdoor shut and painted in his bedroom.

———

I supposed my life was over. On Monday at school, I couldn't even look Royce McNabb's way. I supposed all his worst fears about me had been realized, and then some. Now he thought I lived in a madhouse with a trigger-happy grandma and snakes and naked—nude women in the attic.

But everybody was in such an uproar, I was lost in the shuffle. People who hadn't even seen her could describe every square inch of Maxine Patch, speeding like Eve, headlong through town on a sunny Sunday afternoon. Augie Fluke said she did the high jump over tree stumps. Ina-Rae didn't know what to think, but knew better than to quiz me about it. Then when we got up for the Pledge of Allegiance, Royce looked back and somehow caught my eye. And he winked. That could have meant anything, of course. But I tried my shy smile again and hoped for the best.

Before that week was out it began to dawn on me that nobody would hold a little excitement against you in a town as quiet as this one. And just as they'd begun to take him for granted, Arnold Green sparked new interest. There was some talk about running him out of town. Various church groups called meetings.

Shamed though she was, Maxine had to go back to work at the post office. From the stamp counter she sent forth word that Arnold Green had deceived her. Her reputation was in ruins, and he'd have to marry her.

I suppose word of this must have reached Grandma.

One night out of the blue, she said to me, "You better have your lady teacher here to supper one night."

I jumped. "Miss Butler?" Here?

Grandma nodded. "She'll be passing out grades pretty soon. You want to keep on the good side of her."

I was already on the good side of her. I got the only A's she gave in English. Grandma didn't tell me to invite Mr. Herkimer, though she well knew how I was doing in math.

"Grandma, do I have to?"

Miss Butler looked startled when I invited her for supper. She was too polite to say no, but she gave me a long look, curious and dubious.

When the evening came, I sat waiting for her in our front room. Grandma had cooked all day, and I was a bundle of nerves.

At the sound of a timid knock, I opened the front door to Miss Butler. She was in her dotted Swiss.

"Well, Mary Alice," she said, "how . . . nice."

Seeing my teacher in our front room was eerie. It was a new experience for Miss Butler too. When I showed her to a chair, her eyes roamed the room. She read Grandma's Souvenir of Starved Rock pillow. She noticed the flat square in the carpet where we'd taken down the stove after winter. Since most of what she'd heard about us Dowdels didn't make for polite conversation, ours drifted.

Grandma loomed suddenly in the door to the

kitchen, in a fresh apron. "Come on in," she boomed at Miss Butler, "and we'll tie the feedbag on you."

Miss Butler quaked.

So did I when I saw the kitchen table. It was set with four places.

Before I could think, Arnold Green stepped up behind us. His horn-rims flashed, and my brain buzzed. Miss Butler was so refined, even prim. And there was talk of running Arnold Green out of town for ruining Maxine Patch. And Grandma had invited him to supper. Oh, Grandma, I thought, what are you up to?

I fumbled over the introductions. "I have heard so much about—I mean, how do you do?" Miss Butler murmured to Mr. Green.

I knew I couldn't eat a bite. But Grandma bustled around our chairs, loading the table. Fried chicken. Mashed turnips. Hominy with stewed tomatoes and a casserole of canned green beans and fatback. Since nothing was ready in the garden, there was a quivering green Jell-O mold. There were corn muffins and cloverleaf rolls. Two kinds of jelly in cut-glass dishes. A decorative butter pat from Cowgills' Dairy Farm. You couldn't see the oilcloth.

"Oh my," murmured Miss Butler, "how . . . much."

But Arnold Green fell to it. He didn't feed this well up at The Coffee Pot Cafe, and he was a starving artist.

Grandma presided from her end of the table, gazing at a gizzard and demolishing a thigh. She piled bones, waiting for the silence to force conversation.

At last, Miss Butler chanced a glance across the groaning table at Arnold Green. I was too young to know how much a dangerous man interests a good woman.

His glasses were steamed from the dinner, so it was hard to catch his eye. But she spoke. "I so admire the artistic temperament."

In silence Grandma loaded a fork with mashed turnip.

Miss Butler had a low, pleasing voice when she wasn't yelling at us in school. "My only talent is appreciation," she said. "I sit at the feet of the Bard."

Arnold Green flickered.

"Indeed, I look up to all men of artistic talent," Miss Butler said, though she was no shorter than Arnold Green. He looked suddenly across cruets at her.

Their eyes met.

Somehow, Grandma knew. In a town like this, an unmarried man was either going to be packed off or picked off. She'd decided against Maxine Patch. She backed Miss Butler.

For the rest of the month until he went back to New York, most evenings found Arnold Green strolling to the Noah Atterberrys'. Miss Butler roomed there. They sat out on the porch swing in full view. At the time I supposed they discussed art and poetry and Paris. He used Vitalis now, and Kreml for his dandruff. Grandma kept him in clean shirts. Public opinion shifted his way. Maxine Patch was fit to be tied.

And I didn't mind too much about Royce. He was friendly enough, but either he was keeping his distance, or I was keeping mine. We'd both been strangers in their midst here, but was that enough? I guessed not and didn't mind too much. Really, not at all, hardly.

Gone with the Wind

Suddenly school was almost out and summer upon us. And I didn't know what to think about that.

We had a stretch of perfect weather, here in the healthiest climate in Illinois. Little red blushes showed down in Grandma's strawberry plants. The hollyhocks were every color. Trees leafed out overnight, and the streets were like tunnels with bright countryside at either end. One magic morning the whole town was scented with lilac.

Spring didn't come to Chicago like this. I went around with a lump in my throat I couldn't account for. Then a letter came from Mother with a postscript from Dad.

We'd written back and forth all year, though of course I didn't tell them everything. Mother always tucked in a stamp for me to use to write back. Joey sent postcards: of a burro in a sombrero, of the Fort Peck dam. One was of the Great Salt Lake with a little bag of real salt sewn to the card. I still have them. Then this letter came from Mother and Dad.

I'd make my way to school every morning lost in thought. By now I knew who lived in every house along the way. I knew this town as I'd never know Chicago.

Graduation was coming, though we were only graduating five: four girls who never spoke to anybody younger, just like in Chicago, and Royce McNabb. They'd chosen their class motto:

WE FINISH—
ONLY TO BEGIN

Now plans were afoot for the all-school party to wind up the year. We'd divided into committees, though Carleen Lovejoy didn't want me on hers. I was one of them now, but I hadn't been born here.

Then, in the midst of an ideal day, the sky outside our classroom windows turned a shade of yellow I'd never seen. We were in Home Ec., and the room stirred. This was one of those times when everybody else knew something I didn't.

The siren on the town water tower suddenly wailed. Mr. Fluke leaned in the door. "Miss Butler, get your girls down the basement, quick as you can."

She laid a hand on her throat. She was wearing an engagement ring now, about an eighth of a carat. Something akin to the end of the world seemed to be happening. It was like evening in here. People were just shapes. I turned to Ina-Rae.

"That's the tornado siren," she said, bug-eyed and already out of her desk. She often looked worried. Now she looked scared. I was petrified. I'd heard about tornadoes, but thought they happened somewhere else. Everybody filed out, so orderly, I didn't know them. Then we were on the stairs to the basement.

Then I'd shied off and was running across the schoolyard, skirttails whipping, Cuban heels pounding. Anybody with good sense was taking cover, but I wanted to go home. A breeze came up. The Coffee Pot Cafe looked empty, and the screen door was beginning to flap.

Hanging pots swayed on people's porches, and it kept getting darker. When I was in sight of home, rain bucketed from every direction. There was Grandma, making her way to the house up the back walk, leaning into the wind. She held something against herself, folded in her apron.

She looked astounded to see me and pointed to the house. The clothesline was twanging, and the wet wind was full of chaff from the fields. We made it to the kitchen, plastered with wet leaves. She sent me down the cellar stairs ahead of her. "Go to the southwest corner."

But I didn't know where it was. Everybody but me knew you always shelter in the southwest corner of the cellar. Tornadoes come from that direction, usually. With any luck, the house will be blown off you, not on you.

She got around me and led the way. I'd never known more about the cellar than I could help. If we had a snake in the attic, who knew what lived down here? It had an earth floor, and it was stacked with jars. I thought of flying glass.

A splintery old deacon's bench was wedged across the southwest corner. Grandma dropped down, breathing hard. I needed to know if we were going to die. In the gloom her gleaming spectacles turned on me.

"What in the Sam Hill did that school send you kids home for?" she said over the whining wind. "They ought to have you under the tables in the school basement."

"I escaped. I wanted to . . . come home."

She could read minds, even in the dark. She knew I'd wanted to make sure she was all right. "I've lived through all of them so far," she said.

But now she was having trouble keeping the bundle in her apron quiet. I felt a paw on my knee as Bootsie stepped from Grandma's lap to mine. Grandma gave up and uncovered April's little green eyes blinking up at us. "Grandma, you saved them."

She shrugged that off. "I happened to be down in the cobhouse when the siren went."

That was a whopper. We both knew it. Bootsie was butting my hand, digging in her claws to find a safe place.

We began to hear more than wind lashing the trees. The air was full of things now, anything loose. "Grandma, are we going to—"

A terrible sound wiped my mind clean. It was like a giant, chattering typewriter directly overhead.

"That'll be the tacks coming out of the tar paper on the roof," Grandma hollered in my ear. "Hoo-boy."

Then a Wabash locomotive came full steam at us, out of the sky. "Here we go," she said. She pushed my head down, and we bent double over the cats. Bootsie froze.

Then sudden silence popped my ears. Not a jam jar jiggled. Years later, seemingly, the siren sounded all clear.

Ordinary gray afternoon fell through the kitchen windows when we got upstairs. Grandma's gardening hat still hung from a chair back. She jammed it on her head, and I followed her out onto the back porch.

A wide strip of tar paper curled down off the eaves. Grandma looked past it to survey the yard. It looked like a light snow had fallen. But it was the shredded blossoms of the snowball bushes. Limbs were everywhere. Grandma told me to take the cats down to the cobhouse. "They shed," she said. "And bring back gum boots, gloves, and a crowbar. And step right along."

Then we were walking through town. I cleared our way through the fallen branches, so I was glad for the gloves. Chimney bricks were everywhere, and lengths of drainpipe, and barrel staves. A voice or two sounded far off from people venturing out. We turned down a street and came to Old Man Nyquist's big corner lot. The barn stood, but there wasn't a leaf on his pecan tree. The front porch and the dog underneath it were missing from his house, and you could see through the roof.

Stepping over lumber, we went around back to get in his kitchen that way. It had been a wreck before the storm—crusty pans in the sink, a sticky, never-scrubbed floor. Grandma examined it to see if it would take her weight.

"He naps," she said, starting up the stairs. Behind the first door was nothing but stack after stack of yellowed newspapers. Behind the second door half the ceiling had come down on a collapsed iron bedstead. And under the bedstead was Old Man Nyquist, pinned.

Haunted eyes bored out of a gaunt, gray face. It looked like we weren't a minute too soon. The crowbar came in handy as we worked like troopers, shifting the bedstead off him. A ton of plaster had fallen on it. We were standing in piles more. At last, Old Man Nyquist rolled free and glared up from the floor. We were all white with plaster dust.

"You old busybody buzzard," he growled at Grandma. "How'd you get in?"

"Your kitchen door's in the yard, you ossified old owl-hoot," Grandma yelled, returning fire. "I come to rob you blind."

He noticed the crowbar. "You would too." He wasn't stone deaf, though he hadn't heard the siren.

Staggering to his feet, he swayed like an ancient, punch-drunk prizefighter. I thanked heaven he napped in his clothes. Crunching over to the window, he looked out.

He squinted hard and turned in triumph. "You'll be hurtin' for pecans this fall!" he bellowed at Grandma.

"Then I'll get me something else you've got," she blasted back. "So keep it nailed down and locked up, you old skinflint."

"Biddy!" he barked.

"Coot!" she replied.

Then we left.

I couldn't wait to get out of there. A block away I said, "Grandma, Old Man Nyquist's *mean*."

She nodded. "Nobody'll go near him. He'd have been wedged under them bedsprings till the next Republican administration."

Nobody'd go near him but Grandma.

We walked on toward the Wabash tracks, keeping an eye out for downed wires. Now I knew where we were heading next. We crossed the tracks and turned past the grain elevator and Veech's garage. Beyond the Deere implement shed we saw Mrs. Effie Wilcox's house still standing, though her front gate hung by a hinge.

But then maybe it always had. I didn't get over on this side of the tracks very often. Bent siding from the implement shed littered her yard, but her porch was still on. Grandma tried not to hurry. You could see most of the house from the front door, but she made free to go inside.

Mrs. Wilcox decorated her living-room walls with

magazine pictures of puppies and people from the Bible. These were all in place. The crocheted antimacassars in variegated colors lay flat on her chair arms.

Mumbling with nerves, Grandma twitched through the rooms. Mrs. Wilcox's bed was made. Grandma looked under it. In the kitchen an uncorked Lydia Pinkham's bottle stood untoppled on the drainboard. But the house was deserted.

"Grandma, are we going to have to look in her cellar?"

"She don't have one." Grandma's brow was furrowed. She glanced out the back door. I couldn't see anything out there, but that was the point. At the end of her garden was a hole in the ground, surrounded by headless jonquils.

Grandma nearly fell back. "Her privy's gone. What if she blew away in it?"

What if she fell in the hole? But I fought the thought. Just the idea of Mrs. Wilcox sailing over the grain elevator in her privy was enough.

The front door squawked behind us. Mrs. Wilcox drifted through her house and appeared in the kitchen, her usual self. She went all over town in an apron and a hat and carpet slippers. Three in her kitchen was a crowd.

"Howdy," she said, focusing on us.

Grandma turned on her. "Effie, where you been?"

Mrs. Wilcox drew in her cheeks, a sight in itself. "Well, I don't like to say."

Grandma's eyes snapped. "I thought you'd blown away in your privy."

"I come close," Mrs. Wilcox said. "When the siren blew, I got behind my pie safe, and I was too nervous to live. Couldn't hardly wait for the all clear. Then I really had to go, but my privy had went."

Grandma rubbed her forehead. "So you wandered off to use somebody else's privy."

"Yours," Mrs. Wilcox said.

We left then, Grandma bustling to prove she hadn't given two hoots about Mrs. Wilcox. But I saw through that. I hadn't lived with her all year for nothing. Sometimes I thought I was turning into her. I had to watch out not to talk like her. And I was to cook like her for all the years to come.

Picking our way through debris, we crossed the tracks at the Wabash depot. The town swarmed with people, assessing the damage. Weirdly, the sun came out. "We got off easy," Grandma remarked.

"Were tornadoes worse when you were a girl?" I asked to test her.

She waved me away. "What we had today was a light breeze. When I was a girl, a tornado hit an outdoor band concert. It twisted the tuba player four feet into the ground like a corkscrew before we could get help to him."

We strolled on in our gum boots, Grandma swinging the crowbar.

"Grandma, is Mrs. Wilcox your best friend?"

"We neighbors," she said.

After Grandma and I got home, we cleaned up the yard, working together till dark.

As Grandma said, we got off easy. The tornado had dealt us a glancing blow. It set down on farmland between here and Oakley, plowing a giant furrow and annihilating a corncrib. But it was all people talked about, so the end of school crept up before we knew it.

I noticed a change in Grandma. Sometimes I couldn't tell whether she was changing or I was. But this time she was. Though never idle, she was a whirling dervish now. She undertook a second bout of spring cleaning, even after she'd rubbed all the finish off the house the first time around. Now that Arnold Green had gone back to New York to await Miss Butler, Grandma turned his mattress and painted all the trim in his room.

I came home one afternoon to find half the contents of the cobhouse out in the yard. I thought the tornado had come back. Grandma was inside with her hair tied up, giving the cobhouse the cleaning-out of its life. She could never throw anything away but a used-up flypaper strip, so she was rearranging. In the yard stood a turning lathe, a shingle machine, a circular saw, and a row of chamber pots from the days when they were decorated with moss roses. Bootsie and April sat up on the back porch, waiting for this to be over.

When I offered to give Grandma a hand, she snapped my head off. "Go on up to the house and study for them exams," she barked. Though we both knew no power on earth would save me in math. But she wouldn't even let me set the table for supper these nights. I took my sweet time figuring out what had come over Grandma.

Then graduation came, with ceremonies in the United Brethren Church. All the town but Grandma was there. After the experience of the Christmas program, Miss Butler decided against pulling a choir together. As president of the board of education, Mr. Earl T. Askew handed out the five diplomas, and Royce McNabb was Valedictorian. He'd won a tuition scholarship to the U. of I. at Champaign.

The all-school party was that night, a hayride and a wienie roast out on the Bowman farm. There weren't enough boys for a prom, and the Baptists and the Methodists didn't dance.

We could fit the whole school on a hayframe, pulled by two mules. Some of us were too shy for a party. The Johnson brothers didn't show up. Then that evening turned out to be a greater disaster than the tornado, if you were Carleen Lovejoy.

On the hayride home Royce and I sat together on the hayframe, back by the lantern, dangling our feet. I don't know how it happened. Call it fate.

"How's things at your house?" Royce hazarded, though he still wasn't much for small talk.

"Don't rub it in," I said.

"No, I think your grandma's a real interesting person," he said, and our hands brushed. "Everybody—"

"Royce, we're lucky she's not here on this hayframe with us. You must have noticed she rarely misses a party. But let's leave her out of this if we can. The moon's out, and Carleen's in a snit because we're sitting together. Let's just enjoy ourselves and have a hayride."

"Are you bossy?" he inquired, lantern light woven into his knitted brows.

"Who, me?" I said. "Maybe a little."

"What would happen if I wrote to you from the U. of I.?"

"I'd faint and fall over from surprise," I said, though somehow his arm had found its way around my shoulder. "There are lots of girls at the U. of I. It's a coeducational institution."

"But what would you do if I did?" he said. "Write, I mean."

"I'd write back," I said. And Ina-Rae, buried in the hay behind us but near enough I could feel her breath on my ear, told Carleen all about it.

When I came in that night with straw in my hair, I knew it was time for a showdown with Grandma. She was in the front room, pretending to be asleep in the platform rocker. As a rule, she had to wake herself up to go to bed. But she was sitting up for me, awake behind her eyelids.

"What?" she said, stirring when I stepped up beside her.

"Grandma, I've been thinking."

"You should have tried that in math class," she observed.

"Grandma, I don't want to go back to Chicago. I want to stay here with you."

She knew, of course. Dad was working now. They'd found an apartment up in Rogers Park. Mother was fixing up the second bedroom for me. They wanted me home as soon as school was out. It was all in the letter.

I wanted to explain to Grandma how she needed me here. I'd fuss about her if I wasn't here to see how she was. But she'd just spent days working herself into the ground to prove I was only in her way. She'd been helping me leave for a week.

"I need your bed," she said. "I'm thinking about running this place as a rooming house. I miss the rent off that little New York feller."

"Grandma."

"Might cook for them and bring in a little extry that way." She was looking aside, out the bay into the dark.

"Grandma, was I too much trouble?"

That went too far. But I was her granddaughter, and she'd taught me everything I knew, and I liked to win.

Her hand came up to her mouth. That big old work-scarred hand with Grandpa Dowdel's gold band embedded in it.

"What would your paw think if I kept you?" she said finally. "I don't want your maw after me."

"Grandma, Mother's terrified of you. She always was. You know that."

"Me?" Grandma was the picture of surprise. "She's from Chicago. I'm nothin' but an old country gal."

She could look at me again now, though her eyes were pink and glistening. "You take the kitten. I'll keep the cat," she said. "You go on home to your folks. It'll be all right. I don't lock my doors."

That meant I could come back whenever I could manage it. And she was telling me to go. She knew the decision was too big a load for me to carry by myself. She knew me through and through. She had eyes in the back of her heart.

Ever After

I was married in Grandma's house, in the front room. It was a sunny day in warm weather. She'd taken down the stove, and the windows of the bay stood open, over the bobbing snowball bushes.

It was in the last year of the war, and you can't imagine how things were then. The war scattered people to the four winds. Joey was flying B-17 Fortress missions over Germany, and so my heart lived in my mouth. Dad was doing war work with Boeing out in Seattle. He and Mother were living there. Travel was next to impossible, so they couldn't be there. Even the bridegroom's family couldn't come to the wedding.

It would have been easier to get married in Chicago. I'd held on to the apartment in Rogers Park and took the El every morning down to the Tribune Tower to my cub reporter job. Those "Newsy Notes" had paid off in time. Though it meant I'd have to ride the wartime version of the Wabash Blue Bird, sitting on my luggage in the aisle, I wanted to be married in Grandma's house.

I'd saved up on my ration card for new shoes and a suit from the basement store at Marshall Field. Though I wore a hat and gloves, I was married bare-legged because you couldn't get nylons by then, for love or money.

Then it was all a last-minute rush because I had to marry my soldier on a three-day pass.

Grandma baked the wedding cake. Sugar was hard to come by, though not for her. She made me a nosegay bouquet to carry—lilies of the valley and Queen Anne's lace from her yard, poked through a paper doily. She wore her floral print with the net collar, the dress she'd worn years ago to the county fair.

Reverend Lutz of the United Brethren Church stood by the platform rocker to perform the ceremony. When he asked who gave the bride away in marriage, Grandma said, "That'd be me."

She handed me over. Then she looked aside, out the bay window, blinking at the brightness of the day. I know because I looked back for one more glimpse of her. Then I married Royce McNabb.

We lived happily ever after.

About the Author

———

Richard Peck, the acclaimed author of over twenty-five novels, has won the prestigious Margaret A. Edwards Award for lifetime achievement in young adult literature. *A Long Way from Chicago,* his prequel to *A Year Down Yonder,* was named a Newbery Honor Book, a National Book Award finalist, an ALA Notable Book, and an ALA Best Book for Young Adults. Mr. Peck grew up in Decatur, Illinois, and now lives in New York City.